I0772971

RICHARD WOLFRAM

MISSION: Remember

Richard Wolfram

ISBN-13: 978-1-965352-10-6

To my grandsons,
Daniel, Jacob, Maxwell, Beckett, and Callum

may you grow in faith and understanding.

Acronyms used

ASAP – as soon as possible
COD – Carrier onboard delivery
K-Bay – Kaneohe Bay, Home of MCBH
MCBH – Marine Corps Base Hawaii
USMC – United States Marine Corps
USAFA – United States Air Force Academy

Chapter One

Water swelled as far as Jake could see. Up and down it moved in about five feet of surf except for the little speck on the horizon. The float support he'd fashioned by tying the legs of his cotton sweatsuit and filling them with air did its job and helped keep him afloat for the moment. USMC Gunny Roars had taught him that trick. "Tie the legs tight and float all night." *Dad prepared me for this.*

The speck became the target Jake decided to swim for, but it was a long way off. He was tired after four hours in the water even though he had the floating support. Reaching the top of the swells, he could see the speck getting larger. The tide carrying him in that direction encouraged him to keep moving toward it. *What a break. The speck looks so far away.* The sun setting behind him kept the glare out of his eyes.

How did I get here and where is here? Jake remembered playing a video game in his bunk on the sailboat. Its movement had rocked him asleep dreaming about his mom's roast beef with a side of carrots and mashed potatoes and gravy until a wave broke and splashed him in the face with eye-stinging saltwater bringing him back to reality. Between playing that video game and the splash of salt water he couldn't remember anything. *Stay calm, observe, and figure it out.*

Salty water meant an ocean somewhere. As he scanned the surface, the water shimmered its depth in a dark shade of turquoise blue. He noticed a fin with a divot cut out of it breaking water 50 yards away and closing on him. He never contemplated becoming a shark's dinner. But given the day's events so far, why not?

He instinctively reached for his ever-present survival knife strapped to the calf of his leg. His hand came up empty. *I'm not going down without a fight.* The shark closed the gap between them to twenty yards and the adrenaline rush Jake felt building readied him for a battle to the death, probably his. He braced himself.

Without skipping a beat, a second fin popped out of the water on the back of the most beautiful dolphin Jake had ever seen. It rammed into the shark, ruining its day, and then danced by Jake chattering up a storm. Suddenly another dolphin broke the surface, then another and another. Jake found himself cocooned by a pod of dolphins. He couldn't believe the luck coming his way. No more shark worries. A dolphin eased right up beside him and Jake grabbed the fin and the dolphin towed him toward the growing speck. *I wonder if it's an island, but it's still a long way off.*

Holding on to the dolphin's fin in the rolling sea began to take its toll on Jake. Every time he rose to the crest of a wave he got a face full of salt water. It looked like even with the help of the tide and the dolphin he wouldn't make it. Between coughing up water with each swell and his eyes burning from the spray, exhaustion would defeat him. Jake began to lose his grip on the dolphin's fin collapsing into the surf in an exhausted state of unconsciousness.

Dreaming or dead, Jake floated in the air looking down on himself lying on a beach. "You're going to be alright," he heard a voice say. "I'm Mic, here to be of service. That's Cal on your left and Ace on your right."

Hearing voices with no one in sight troubled Jake. "Who's there?"

"We were sent from another place to ensure your good health and help you see a purpose beyond this life," the voice said. "We serve as your guardians. Cal made sure the knots on your trouser legs were tight. I sped up the tide flow to get you to shore sooner. Ace directed dolphins to deflect the shark, cocoon you, and taxi you toward the island. Cal and I intervened when you lost consciousness and deposited you at the water's edge on the shore of the island."

"So, I'm not dead?" Jake continued to look for the source of the voice.

"Do you see that shimmering wrinkle that looks like a heat wave over there to the north?" the voice asked.

"Shimmering wrinkle! I don't see it any more than I see you or anyone else."

"I can fix that," another voice said. Instantly Jake saw two angelic beings on either side of him with hands on his shoulders and a third floating in front of him, pointing to what appeared to be a shimmering wrinkle in the sky.

"I take it you're Mic."

"Yes, and that wrinkle separates here from there," Mic said. "One day, *there* will be here as well, but until then, we serve the One who is making it happen."

Jake didn't know what to think about that any more than he understood how he was looking down at himself. He pointed to himself on the beach. "How can I be here when I'm there?" To his left Cal snickered. "Remember what Mic said referring to 'there.'"

"There isn't 'there'," Ace said, "It's there." He pointed at the wrinkle.

"You almost lost your life in the water," Mic went on. "Our task is to make sure you live for another day. You are only aware of us because of your current subconscious dream state. You must learn about yourself and Him whom we serve. We are here to help you learn and keep you alive for the moment."

"For the moment? What does that mean?"

"Your best future is tied to Him whom we serve. But there are no guarantees. You are the wild card. He wants you to understand '*there*,'" Mic pointed to the shimmer, "and have access for yourself and the others."

"What others?"

"The ones He will give access because of your influence. But more about that another time. For now, you sleep."

Chapter Two

Beads of sweat rolled down her forehead just like yesterday and every day since the first. A lovely and majestic sunrise came up over the eastern side of the island. Sandy breathed in the warm ocean air. Some unseen force pulled her along up the beach on the western side of the island.

She had been stranded on this island since the day a tsunami capsized her father's fishing boat a year ago. She hadn't seen her father since that day. She couldn't explain what had kept her afloat and helped her body surf right to the shallows of the island shore. Probably, no one knew where the tsunami had taken the boat or even that she had survived.

Her years of fishing with her father and camping with him in the Australian outback had equipped her with survival skills. She figured that, coupled with Godly assistance kept her alive and well fed.

Exploring the island, she found indigenous fruit trees supplying her with bananas, mangos, papayas and bread fruit. Palm trees swayed with coconuts, and assorted roots and wild berries grew here and there. As an additional plus, she found an occasional egg or two from birds. Fish and clams were abundant. Plenty of fresh water flowed from the interior streams and lake. She thanked God every day for the abundance, and especially that her Swiss army knife in her pocket had survived with her. All in all, surviving here hadn't been difficult, thank God.

In the middle of so much beauty she missed people. She missed her father. Not knowing if he'd survived or not brought her the greatest anxiety. Especially today. As far as she could tell, today should be Sunday. She and her father would always find a way to worship on Sunday wherever they were. They took time to tell God thanks for their blessings great or small. They would sing a favorite hymn or song and knew that God was always with them. She liked to hum a tune or sing a song as she foraged for food around the Pacific paradise. If only someone else could sing with her.

"It sure would be nice to be found today on my birthday," she said. "At least I think today is my birthday."

She kicked at the sand. "Lord, what are you waiting for? We talk every day, all day some days. But I can't figure out why I'm still here. What's your plan?"

At that moment a coconut fell from the palm tree ahead of her. She heard it hit with a plop in the sand just beyond a sand dune and, considering it a birthday present for her lunch, went to retrieve it. She crested the dune and her eyes widened to the still form lying in the sand. A figure lay there, clad only in boxers and a T-shirt, with what appeared to be his pants around his chest with the legs tied in knots. She moved closer to see if he had a pulse all the while remembering the paramedic training she had begun at her community college. *My unit in first aid training covered this sort of thing.*

Yes, his heart beat with a solid rhythm. She gently shook him, but he made no response. Unconscious or sleeping too soundly from exhaustion she surmised. It appeared from the tide marks he had been there a good part of the night. Now with the sun coming over the trees he would need shade to avoid a bad sunburn. The boy looked muscular and strong probably a head taller than her. Not a good idea to try and move him without knowing the extent of his injuries. Instead, she grabbed several palm branches and weaved a palm blanket to cover him.

* * *

What is that sound? Jake shook his head trying to wake up. *Where am I?*

He heard ocean waves crashing against the sandy shore and he could swear he heard a beautiful voice humming a light and airy tone. Something familiar from his younger days came to mind, but he couldn't place it. Opening his eyes the brightness made him squint. Through the glare he spotted her shapely silhouette a few yards away standing at the water's edge where the gentle waves rippled over her feet. He noticed the covering of palm fronds over him shielding from the midday sun.

"Where am I?" Jake croaked. The salt water from his swim and lying in the sand all night had left him parched and dry. The girl heard him and came over offering water in a coconut shell. "I thought you might be thirsty," she said.

After a cool drink, Jake sat up. He stretched his arms and legs relieving the stiffness. The hoarseness in his throat remained but left him no worse for the wear. When he looked up, he found himself looking into the most captivating blue eyes he had ever seen surrounded by a tanned face and golden hair. He pulled his pants from around his neck and worked at untying the knots he'd tied in the legs. *Cal didn't have to tighten them so tight.*

"I'm not sure how I got here," he said. "I remember being in the water miles out west of here. This island looked like a speck. I couldn't see anything else, so I tried to swim for it. It's a long story." He didn't want to tell her about sharks, dolphins, and the tide. She might think he suffered from delirium. Besides, he didn't know if he believed what Mic told him about how he had gotten to shore, so what could he say? He certainly couldn't mention Mic and his two companions.

"I ended up stranded here after my dad's fishing boat was sunk by a tsunami," the girl said. "Also, a long story. On my walk this morning a coconut led me to see you lying here. I thought it best not to try and move you since I didn't know if you were injured. I threw the palm blanket sunscreen together for you. Now that you are awake how do you feel? Are you hurt anywhere?" she asked.

"Other than my throat, I feel okay," Jake croaked. "Could I have some more of that water? I'm probably a little dehydrated."

She offered Jake the shell again. After he guzzled the remaining water, she took the shell and got up and headed for the trees.

She looked back as she left. "I'm Sandy. Just relax and I'll bring some more water for you. Some fruit too." Then she disappeared into the trees.

Jake laid the palm blanket aside and slipped his pants over his feet. As he stood to pull them up, he took a roll in the sand. Shaking his head he slowly stood again. This time equilibrium returned. He grabbed his pants and decided to wade out into the water to rinse off the sand that he and they were covered in. The water invigorated him by cooling his core temperature. It also rinsed the sand out of his hair and body crevices replacing them with a saltwater sheen.

Back on the beach he wrung out his pants and laid them on the palm blanket to dry. Plopping down beside them, he took in the view. *What a beautiful scene. Sandy beach, ocean waves and an intriguing girl. Can this day get any better?*

Jake watched the waves breaking against the shore.

"Here you go," the girl said, startling him. Jake hadn't noticed her come back through the trees. "Fresh water and fruit for lunch. Just what the doctor ordered." She had a coconut shell full of water and a papaya and banana in her hands.

She handed the shell of water to him.

"Now that you're not caked in sand you remind me of some of the boys back home except for your accent. You're the first person I've seen in over a year. I talked with God earlier about how nice it would be to have someone find me today since it's my birthday. Except for the fact that I found you, you're probably the answer to my prayer."

"I don't know about that," Jake responded, "but here we are. Where are we?"

"I'm not exactly sure. I'm guessing we are somewhere in the south pacific, east of New Zealand," she replied.

"Wow." After he thought about it for a moment Jake looked up at her and smiled. "If I have to be stranded somewhere, this seems as good a place as any. You seem nice too. How about that fruit?"

She handed him the papaya. His stomach grumbling reminded him he hadn't eaten anything in the last 24 hours. He bit into the juicy fruit sucking in the nectar. Sweet and tasty, it hit the spot.

She handed him the banana with a smile. Jake went after the stem end without much luck.

"Try the other end," she instructed. "I notice that most people automatically try to open a banana at the stem end, but the tail end can be easier." He took her advice and the banana was good too.

Jake finished off the water in the coconut shell. *Another papaya would be nice.*

"You know, I try not to make it a habit of entertaining young men with no pants on. Put them on, and I'll show you where some fruit trees are."

"I try not to make it a habit of dressing in front of strangers," Jake responded.

"Well, I told you I'm Sandy," she replied as she turned toward the trees.

"I know you are. So is everything else around here… Oh, I get it. Your name is Sandy. I'm Jake," he said shaking his head, embarrassed that he missed her name the first time. He stood up, slipped on his pants, and they headed for the trees.

Chapter Three

Jake watched Sandy as he followed her into the tree line. Strong and athletic, she moved with an easy confidence that impressed him. She wore cutoff shorts and a sleeveless top. Both fit her well. He had to admit Sandy was a beautiful girl. Since he didn't know where he was going, he was content to follow along behind her, for now.

Not far into the trees, they started up a slow incline. As they reached the crest, he noticed a waterfall spilling into a pool of water. Several fruit trees rimmed the pool. He picked a papaya and enjoyed it like the first. It tasted sweet and left juice running down his chin. He'd never tasted fruit like this before.

"It's kind of like heaven on earth," Sandy said. "God has supplied us with food to eat, water to drink, and a gorgeous day. And now I even have someone to talk with. Life is good."

"I hate to burst your bubble, but I don't buy into that God stuff. This island is here. There is fruit and water on it. You're here because of a freak wave. Now I'm here, which is a mystery to me. But that's it."

"Agree to disagree," Sandy replied. "If I hadn't come upon you when I did, you would be sporting a really good sunburn. But God arranged for me to find you and prevent that from happening. Besides that, you have no idea how you got to the beach. I say it's a God thing."

"I don't see it," Jake said. "I do agree that this place is great. Have you explored it all?"

"Most of it. I'll be happy to give you a tour another day. Help yourself to a good drink from the falls. It's clean and drinkable. Then I need to get going. The sun will be setting soon, and I want to get back to my shelter. You're welcome to join me if you feel up to it. It's a bit of a hike, though."

"Lead on," Jake said.

They left the pool of water and waterfall by another path that had them at the beach a little further south from where they had been. As they followed the shoreline, they came to a rocky outcropping. Sandy turned inland and walked past a pile of driftwood that appeared to be a potential signal fire. Just into the tree line Jake noticed a platform raised about two feet off the ground. Four palm trees stood as corner posts with a bamboo frame lashed up in the middle. The bed consisted of bamboo laid across the frame, covered with palm branches and palm leaves. A bamboo pole lashed above the platform provided for a lean-to effect with palm branches laid from it to one edge of the platform.

"It's not much but it's home for now," Sandy said. "There is also a cave a little further up that I go to during storms. I spend most of my time around here when I'm not exploring."

Another grounded lean-to ten feet from the platform covered a good size pile of driftwood and deadwood that Jake figured was for fires since the firepit was about five feet in front of it. It was a nice firepit too. A three-foot circle of assorted rocks on the outside, surrounded a small teepee of firewood ready to light in the center. He wondered what Sandy did for fire starter.

"What would you like for dinner?" Sandy asked. "Fish or clams or both?"

"Whatever is easiest."

Sandy walked over to the rock wall and grabbed two spears made from bamboo. "Let's go," she said heading for the water.

Just south of the camp beyond a rocky ledge, a tide pool had formed. Sandy handed him one of the spears and walked into the pool about knee deep. "The trick to spearing a fish is to remember that light bends in the water. Where you see the fish isn't really where they are. You have to adjust your throw to compensate for that."

Slowly Sandy raised her spear and then threw it. The churning water told Jake she got one. Sandy walked to the spot and picked up the spear. Sure enough, there was a fish stuck on the end of it. "It's a nice herring," she said. "A couple more of these will make a nice dinner. Don't just stand there, give it a try."

Jake walked into the water and looked for fish.

"Just stand still for a moment and wait for one to swim by."

He watched the water around him and then spotted one. Raising the spear, he let it fly and missed.

"Remember it's closer than it looks."

He retrieved the spear and stood still again to watch. Sandy stood about twenty feet from him when she threw her spear again. "Another herring," she said. "One more will do it. Or a nice clam or two."

Jake refocused on the water around him. He could see a submerged rock a few feet away and threw at it for target practice. He missed it by about six inches. Using that as a frame of reference he mentally adjusted for his next throw. A fish swam by five feet away and Jake threw the spear short of it and to his complete surprise he hit it. "Woohoo," he yelled. "I speared my first fish." He picked up the spear with a fish on the end and brought it to shore laying it next to Sandy's two.

Sandy said, "The clams can wait for another time. That's plenty of herring for dinner."

Using her knife Sandy quickly filleted the three fish. A large flatter rock on the edge of the outcropping made a nice table on which she skinned the filets. "There," she said. "They are all ready to cook unless you like them raw." She took the fish remains further down the beach and put them on some rocks. "The birds will make quick work of them," she said. She picked up the filets and headed back to the camp.

Leaning over the firepit Sandy pulled out a wad of dried grass. Inside the firepit ring she grabbed a fist-sized rock that looked like quartz and a blackish piece that Jake guessed to be flint. She used the rock to strike the flint and threw sparks into the grass, catching it on fire. She used it to ignite the tinder in the middle of the wood teepee. The dry wood of the teepee ignited within seconds. Her fire making expertise impressed Jake.

"Let's go get the rest of what we need," Sandy said. Jake followed her further into the trees. She stopped several times to cut some small branches that were pinky finger round and three feet long. She cut six in total. They walked further and came to a stream. Near it were some giant clam shells and a papaya tree. They each picked a papaya and filled a shell with water and went back to the camp.

Sandy carved points on the branches, placed two in each filet and positioned them over the coals of the fire. "Sit down and relax. The fish won't take long to cook."

Chapter Four

It's been more than thirty-six hours since Jake's last call or text. Concern gnawed in Karen Huber's mind. *It's not like him to miss an evening check-in.* Her smart and considerate son knew how much she appreciated being updated on his status whenever he went away on one of his "missions" learning/training/adventuring. *He must have gotten caught up with something and lost track of time. At 16, he's just like his father was on a mission, focused on it.*

Jake shared everything with her. He told her he thought it cool how his dad's Marine friends worked with him, teaching him all sorts of things. That became especially true over the last year since Stu had passed. He considered his top options for college to be the Naval Academy and the Air Force Academy. He said either would put him in an environment where he could thrive. That's what had him away this time. He crewed on a three masted schooner. It was part of a sailing school in the Pacific south of Australia. They had satellite access and Jake usually called in the evening when his shift ended. *Why hasn't he called?* Karen tried to remain calm.

———•●•———

The fish dinner tasted great and hit the spot for Jake. Sandy turned out to be a good open fire cook. She had soaked the fillets with some of the papaya juice and smoked them over the coals. Paired with mango and banana for dessert Jake found himself full.

A beautiful sunset appeared in the western sky and Jake began to scan the area for a place to sleep. While he could just lay on the beach, survival training taught him it would better to be elevated off the ground. "Any thoughts where I should spend the night?"

"You could sleep where I slept the first night I arrived here. I pulled together a makeshift bed of bamboo and palm leaves just over there," she said pointing up the shore to the north. "Come on I'll show you."

They walked about fifty yards up the beach and then to the tree line. There Jake saw her first bed up about a foot off the ground. "Not too shabby," he said.

"We can refresh the palm leaves and weave a blanket and you'll be all set. If you'd like a fire nearby, I can bring some coals from the firepit and get one started here. But it's going to be a warm night and I haven't noticed any varmints around lately. You probably don't need one."

Jake thought about it and decided to skip the fire. He didn't want to take a chance getting up in the dark and stepping on hot coals on his way to a nature call.

Jake and Sandy worked together to get the bed and blanket ready and then headed back to sit by the fire for a while.

"Where do you live when you're not lost at sea?" Sandy asked.

"My mom and I live on the north shore of Oahu. My dad, Stu, retired from the Marine Corps (United States Marine Corps) as a Master Gunnery Sargent. He considered that his second most important accomplishment."

"What was most important?"

"He said it was marrying my mom and having me for a son. He loved his duty at the Marine base at Kaneohe. That's where he last served so when he retired, we stayed. A year ago, he died in a car wreck. It's hard to believe a guy with thirty years of Marine Corps duty including lots of combat time would be killed in a freak accident like that."

"I'm sorry," Sandy said. "That must have been tough on both you and your mom."

"I really miss him. But my dad's Marine buddies reached out to us and took care of anything we needed. My dad and his Marine buddies always challenged me to grow and learn. They told me they were teaching me skills I would need to survive in a world becoming more hostile and violent every day. They also told me when your time's up, that's it. My dad's dead. So, I just keep on keeping on. What about you? What's your story?"

"I ended up shipwrecked here," Sandy said. "About a year ago my dad and I were fishing south of Australia, his home base. He loved fishing. That's how he made a living. Out of nowhere a tsunami came and flipped the boat, throwing me overboard. By the grace of God, I ended up on the beach of this island. I don't know where the boat went down or what happened to my dad. I don't know if he's even still alive. Every day I pray that he is and God is watching out for him."

"You can keep the God stuff for yourself. I bet you are a good swimmer and that's how you got here."

"I remember feeling exhausted and going under. The next thing I knew I woke up on the beach." Jake figured Mic and Cal would say they had something to do with that.

"I call it a God thing," Sandy said. "There's no other explanation. Besides, God and I go way back. He's never let me down and is always with me just like today. Since we're stuck here together maybe I'll have an opportunity to introduce you to Him."

"How can you believe in a God that lets you get ship-wrecked and lost at sea? That doesn't make any sense."

"There's a lot more to it than that. God didn't cause what happened to me or you. This world and everyone on it have been out of sorts with God since the very beginning when Adam and Eve disobeyed Him. All the bad and evil stuff that goes on is the result of that act of disobedience. It had a lasting effect on everything and everyone. It's a bad news situation with a good news ending. God loved us so much that He provided a way back to himself."

Jake yawned and stretched.

"You must be tired. Why don't we call it a night. I usually get up at first light and go for a swim. You're welcome to join me."

"Sounds good," Jake said, heading off to his makeshift cot. "Good night. Don't let the bed bug's bite."

"Not to worry," Sandy said, walking toward her

platform bed in the trees. "Strangely enough I haven't been bothered by many bugs."

——•●•——

Jake rubbed his eyes and stretched again. Lying there thinking about his conversation with Sandy and her God stuff. He considered that Ace might be responsible for keeping the bugs away from Sandy. *Maybe it's another of Sandy's God things.* He fell asleep contemplating that.

Up aloft in the night sky, Jake's dream or vision continued. He looked down on himself as he had at the beach earlier in the day. Mic on one side of him and Cal on the other, each had a hand on one of his shoulders.

Mic said, "We are here to help you see what you have not seen and cannot see."

"What are you talking about?" Jake asked.

Mic continued. "Do you remember when you were five years old and running around in the forest near the house where you lived, a place your parents told you to never go by yourself?" "Kind of," Jake replied.

"Do you remember what happened?" Mic asked. "You and your friend crossed the road that you weren't supposed to cross and went exploring."

"That's right. We explored in the trees and got turned around. We didn't know which way to go. My friend Bob saw a rabbit that seemed to wink at us and we decided to follow it. We didn't realize it led us deeper into the forest. The trail we followed led us right into a man dressed in camouflage. The man called himself Michael. He carried a bow so we thought he might be a hunter. He looked at us and smiled and asked if we were okay. Bob explained to him how we got lost. We didn't have any food or water. I told him we lived near the base and had crossed the road there into the woods.

Michael gave us a drink from his canteen and told us to follow him. We hiked for a while and then he stopped and pointed to a two-track. "Follow that," he said. "It ends at a black top. Go left and it will take you to the road that you crossed not far from the base. Hurry along because it will be dark soon. You don't want your parents to worry."

Jake said, "Two five-year-old's following a two-track through a forest might cause some to be alarmed. But we were adventurous and now had a plan to get home safely. As we parted, Michael told us God would keep us safe and off we went. When I got home my mom let me have it. She reminded me that she did not want me to cross that road. She busted my butt and restricted me to the house and yard for a week."

"Wait a minute," Jake said. "Michael, Mic, you? You were the hunter who showed us the way."

"Yes, the hunter and I are one and the same. He appointed me your guardian before you were born. He has a plan for you. Cal, Ace and I are to help you see and learn. That's why you are here."

"You mean this He is responsible for me being stranded here?" Jake asked. "Just who is He?"

"He is the One who placed eternity within us," Mic said. "Physical death is not the end of life. His desire is that all people live with Him forever on a new earth. He provides the way for that to happen. But there are forces at work to prevent it. He chose you as His agent to assist some in arriving. He sends us from there to here to be of service in that."

"What a load of bull," Jake said. "Next, you'll tell me that Ace really is in charge of bug control. I don't know how you expect me to believe a story like that."

"There are many who do," Mic replied. "Gunny Roars, your mother and father, and Sandy to name a few. They have heard this truth from eyewitnesses and the Truth has set them free to believe it. For now, just think about it."

Chapter Five

"Wake up sleepy head," Jake heard Sandy say as she shook his shoulder. "It's the start of a beautiful day and time for a swim!" Sandy ran down to the water and dove in.

Jake watched her hit the waves and then got up and found a nearby tree. After he finished his business he went in the water after her. As a strong swimmer, he tried to catch her, but she was out in front and there was no way he could. Instead, swimming along the shore and parallel with her he watched her glide through the surf with strength and ease. *What a beautiful picture of grace.*

There it was again. The fin with the divot. The shark suddenly came up behind Sandy where she couldn't see it.

"Look out," Jake yelled. "Behind you."

Sandy didn't hear Jake yell as she swam. The shark closed in fast. Jake watched the scene unfold in front of him helpless to do anything. He continued to yell and wave his arms all to no avail. He thought Sandy was shark bait for sure. But then to his complete surprise Sandy stood ankle deep on a sand bar that seemed to come out of nowhere and the shark turned out to sea.

Jake remembered what the three had told him about their interventions. *Ace must feel good about his new artwork of underwater sand hills created with the help of the earlier tides.* Sandy, with Jake's prompting, finally noticed the shark swimming away. It didn't seem to bother her.

A pod of dolphins attracted Jake's attention as it swam by. He swam towards them. *Could they be the same ones that rescued me?* Sandy dove in and headed their way. Soon Jake enjoyed a little play time with the dolphins and Sandy. *What a way to start the day!*

Back on the beach Jake told Sandy about the shark encounter he had experienced during his swim to the island. "The shark this morning had the same divot in its dorsal fin." Jake wanted Sandy to know of his concern.

"I swim in this lagoon every day and I've never seen a shark."

"You wouldn't have seen it today if not for the sand bar that saved you. And me pointing it out," Jake replied.

"I've never come across that sand bar before either. It must be a God thing."

"Hah! It's more like a tide thing moving the sand around."

"Agree to disagree," Sandy said. "Let's leave it at that for now. Besides, I'm hungry. How about some fruit for breakfast?"

"Sure, I've worked up an appetite. I'd like a repeat of the papaya and banana and some cool water. Shall I call room service? Or shall we go and sit pool side?"

"Pool side sounds like a good idea," Sandy said. "Let's go."

Jake let Sandy walk ahead, falling in behind her as she led the way into the trees toward the pool of water from the day before. Her wet skin glistened in the sunlight. He sensed an aura around her that intrigued him. Relief swept over him that the shark hadn't harmed her in any way. God thing or not, he would keep an eye on her.

They finished their fruit and water and laid back on the edge of the pond taking in the beauty of the waterfall. Jake looked at Sandy and compared her to every girl he ever met. No one compared. Her beauty reminded him of a flowery meadow on a late spring morning with a soft, fragrant breeze. Her strength and intelligence coupled with her confidence made her quick on her feet. No girl could top her, but for one thing.

"Sandy, tell me more about your 'God thing' stuff. My dad getting killed in a car wreck didn't make sense to me. It still doesn't. My dad, a good guy, a great father and an outstanding Marine always said, 'Marines and God go together like spit and polish.' If there is a God, He wouldn't have let him die like that. My dad talked with me about God often. But since his death I can't believe it."

Sandy probably saw the pain in Jake's eyes. "I pray God will help me say what you need to hear," she said. "And say it in a way that reflects His love and strength for you."

Sandy looked Jake square in the eyes and said, "Have you ever heard it said that God is love?"

"As a kid I remember my mom saying that all the time. Then Jake remembered what Mic had told him about being lost in the forest. *I bet Mic has a big smile on his face right now. He would know what a loving way Mom had with me. He would know that with a mom like her, I would experience what I needed to learn. He wants those memories to help me understand His love and move me closer to Him.*

"Have you ever thought about what 'God is love' means?" Sandy asked. "God is love means nothing can come from him but love. He loves me. He loves you. In fact, he loves everyone. So, when something happens that isn't loving it isn't of God. It's from sin and Satan. That might sound too simple, but it really is simple. You just need to understand it in the context of life from the beginning."

"From the beginning of what?" Jake asked.

"From the beginning of the world. I believe what it says in the Bible that in the beginning God created everything. When He completed His creating, He looked at everything and it was good. It was all perfect. Adam and Eve, the first two people He made were good and perfect too. They had a perfect life in a perfect place that the Bible called the Garden of Eden. God loved them and provided everything they needed to live."

"Yeah, yeah. I heard all that from my mom and church as a boy."

Sandy continued, "It's important to understand the beginning so you can understand God's love. A lot of people think wrongly because of that lack of insight. Many don't understand that there are evil forces at work against God and His love in the world. Forces that cause every kind of pain and discomfort imaginable. Forces responsible for sickness and death and heartache. Those forces came into being after God created His perfect world."

"If that's true," Jake replied, "and only good can come from God, and God made everything perfect, then where did the evil forces come from?"

"That's an age-old question that many people have asked," Sandy said. "God's Word tells us that an angel called Satan wanted to be on an equal level with God and rebelled against Him. He and his follower angels were kicked out of heaven to roam the earth. The ones who remained loyal to God will be with him forever serving Him as He desires."

"So, angels serve God," Jake said. *That agrees with what Mic, Ace and Cal said.*

Sandy said, "Satan, through a snake, tempted Adam and Eve with the same idea of being more like God by eating fruit from a tree that God had told them not to eat. They ate and the perfect relationship Adam and Eve had with God broke and resulted in them being cursed and kicked out of the Garden. The whole world received the curse."

"I guess that doesn't exactly answer the question but it's all the Bible says about it," Sandy said. "Someday when I'm with Jesus I might ask him about it."

"So, you're telling me that I can't hold God responsible for my dad's death? A true God could have stopped it, couldn't He?"

"Death is the result of the broken relationship with God that Adam and Eve brought about because they went against God's will. The Bible calls that sin. Sure, God could have prevented your dad's death. But He didn't. Only He knows why. What I do know is that God uses situations like that for His loving purposes. I know this because of God's response to Adam and Eve after they rebelled against Him. Their punishment matched the result of the rebellion. It brought about physical and spiritual death, and painful labor in making a living and in childbearing. But He also gave them a promise that He would make their relationship right again by sending a descendant of Adam and Eve who would destroy Satan and sin and death."

"Wow!" Jake said. "I've heard some of that before but never in a way that I could understand. I need to think about it."

"There's more I can tell you, but God has blessed us with such a beautiful day. Let's go for a walk."

Sandy grabbed Jake by the hand and pulled him up. "Let me show you behind the waterfall," she said, as she angled up a path that went alongside the falls. Cresting the hilltop the eastern side of the island unfolded for Jake to see. A gentle downward slope of trees and floral vegetation ended with the eastern shore of the island. The beauty matched the guide.

Sandy continued to walk in front. She knew her way through the trees toward the beach even without a pathway. As they cleared the tree line, a flowery meadow spread before them. Jake reached down and picked a little yellow flower with several inches of stem. He ran up to Sandy and tapped her on the shoulder. When she turned, he showed it to her and said, "A beautiful flower for a beautiful girl." He slid it into her golden hair over her ear with a big smile.

"Thank you. It's a Desert Flame, one of my favorites." Jake could tell she hadn't experienced that kind of attention from a boy. He noticed her blushing. With a smile she turned and continued down the hill.

The midday sun overhead and the warm ocean breeze had Jake thinking a quick dip in the ocean would feel good. He ran past Sandy across the beach and into the surf diving into the waves. His pants slowed him down and he decided they needed to be turned into cutoffs to optimize his swimming.

Sandy sat down in the sand, dangling her feet in the water. Jake swam for a while and then sat down next to Sandy.

"You are a strong swimmer. I'm impressed how well you move through the water."

"I love the water," Jake said. "I took a water survival course with my dad's Marines and passed with no problem."

"How about if we walk the beach back to camp? It will take us around the southern end of the island and get us back in time to get some food ready for supper."

Jake's stomach growled at the thought of food.

"Let's go," Jake agreed.

Chapter Six

The south end of the island turned out to be as picturesque as the rest. A beautiful beach crept up into the tree line. The ocean stretched in all directions with no other land in sight. The breeze was soft and warm with a fresh smell that reminded him of recent days spent crewing on the sailboat.

"How did I end up in the water two days ago," Jake wondered out loud. "How did I get from a bunk on a sailboat to treading water with no memory of what happened. It's the weirdest thing."

"I don't know what to tell you," Sandy said. "But I do know that God works in mysterious ways. I think He's up to something with you, and me and this island. I talked with Him about it last night and again this morning. He'll answer in His time."

"Time, we have plenty of. Let me know if He answers you. Although my skepticism about Him continues."

"You could talk with Him yourself. He wants everyone to."

"I don't know what to say. Talking to myself doesn't make sense to me."

"You can talk to him just like you talked to your

father," Sandy said. "That's what He is, your heavenly father. As your heavenly Father, he loves you even more than your dad and can't wait to hear from you. If you could talk to your father right now, what would you say to him?"

"I'd be so glad to talk with him. I miss him. I'd tell him about surviving here on this island. And I'd ask him for help to get someone to find us."

"You told me he died believing. I know that he is with God now in spirit and soul along with everyone else who died believing. I call that heaven 1.0. You can have that same relationship too. God wants it for you. You can have a conversation with God like you were talking with your earthly dad."

"Maybe," Jake said. "I don't know."

"We are about halfway around," Sandy said. They had walked for an hour and a half. "Do you want to spear a couple of fish for supper like we did yesterday? We could plan on digging some clams tomorrow."

"Ok," Jake said as a shiny object caught his eye in the surf. "I wonder what that could be. Do you see it?"

"Probably just a water reflection. I see some dolphins playing out there. Maybe it's light reflected off them."

"No. Something there below the surface reflects the sunlight every time it hits the crest of a wave. Come on, let's go check it out," Jake said heading toward the water.

Sandy followed along right behind him. They swam out toward the reflection through the rolling surf to the break water. The large object floated about 50 yards further out. Jake thought he recognized the dolphins as the same ones that helped him and Sandy with the shark. *Could Cal be using the dolphins to push the object toward the shore?* Swimming closer, Jake recognized an abandoned ship dry bag that looked like the ones on the sailing boat he had been training on. The size of a large duffel bag, it floated because of airtight inner bags.

"I've seen some strange things float into the shore but never anything this large," said Sandy. "Let's pull it in and take a look."

At the shore, Jake lifted the bag out of the water and carried it up on the beach. He recognized the name stenciled on it. "*Legacy*, the name of the boat I trained on. How did this bag end up in the water?"

Sandy stared at the bag. "I bet either the Legacy ran into trouble, or you came up missing and they threw this bag overboard hoping it and you would find each other. That would be a long shot."

"I know what's in this bag. My crew training involved familiarization with its contents and knowing how to use it in an emergency. Let's take it back to camp and unpack it after we take care of this growling stomach of mine."

Jake picked up the bag, throwing it up on his shoulder and continued toward the camp.

"I bet you wonder what's in here," Jake said as he and Sandy walked side by side toward their camp.

"I know it has things to help with survival at sea, probably some food and water."

"There's food and water, a first-aid kit, and a whole lot more. Wait till you see."

As they walked, Jake continued to watch the waves for anything else that might be afloat.

An hour later they arrived at the camp. Jake

dropped the bag near the firepit. Sandy grabbed two spears and they headed to the tidal pool. It didn't take long and they were sitting by the fire eating fish and fruit like the evening before talking about the day's events.

Jake leaned back against the sand. "I've been on this island two plus days and I have to say I've never experienced anything as great as this. The Legacy training turned out to be rigorous and safety oriented. I would call island survival here a piece of cake compared to it. I just can't figure out how I ended up in the water."

"Our minds can block memories that are painful or cause us emotional stress," Sandy said. "Could be your experience. I'll pray that you can remember what happened. In the meantime, let's open that survival bag. I'm going to pretend like it's Christmas and the bag is our present."

Jake unzipped the bag and rattled off the inventory of what it contained. Opening the flap and then breaking the seal on the watertight liner gave access to its contents. Jake pulled out a small Bible.

"Oh wow! Let me see it." Sandy took the small book and after quickly flipping through it held it over her heart. With tearful eyes she began singing, "Praise God from whom all blessings flow, praise Him all creatures here below..."

Jake remembered hearing his mom sing the same words and tune when she took him to church as a boy. He grinned watching Sandy doing a happy dance around the fire, singing her praise to God. The fire made her blue eyes sparkle like the stars. *What a beauty*. Yet, he couldn't figure out why all the excitement over a little book. He didn't know if God existed or not. One thing for sure, Sandy believed He did and showed it.

Jake examined the rest of the bag's contents. He checked everything and the inventory was complete with signaling devices, a first aid kit, basic survival gear like a knife, rope, space blankets and more. In the morning, he would unpack it all in the daylight and show it to Sandy.

Feeling tired, he got up and said, "You must be the happiest person I know. I've never known anyone to react to a little book like you did. Just wait until you see what else comes out of the Christmas bag tomorrow." Jake yawned and stretched. "Time for a little shut eye. I will see you in the morning for a swim. Sweet dreams."

"I'm going to read for a little while until the fire burns low. Talk with God for a bit and then call it a night. What a great day in the Lord. You sleep good too."

Jake smiled at her and headed up the beach to his bed. The light sea breeze scented by the ocean reminded him of home. A magnificent array of stars covered the sky. He knew many by name from his navigation training. He stretched out on the palm leaf bed. Thoughts of his conversations with Sandy about God swirled in his mind as sleep overtook him.

———•●•———

Floating in the night sky, Jake looked down at himself, asleep. *I must be dreaming.*

"You have many questions," Mic said, startling Jake. "We will show you the answers in part."

At that, Jake noticed Ace and Caleb come along side of him and the four of them floated toward the mysterious wrinkle in the sky Jake had seen yesterday beyond Mic. Passing through the wrinkle, a majestic blinding white light greeted Jake. A countless number of people also all bright and white surrounded the light. The intensity and brightness caused him to close his eyes and bow his head. Yet, in his heart a warmth and peace he'd never experienced before embraced him. The soothing nature of it all relaxed him. Then he heard his name.

"Jake, my child, I love you. I made you mine through the water. Remember."

The soft voice emanated from the center of the brightness with joyous laughter that pulled Jake toward it.

"He is the alpha and the omega, the first and the last," proclaimed Mic speaking with a voice of power and awe. "He is the Lamb of God. He is Jesus. You feel His pull because He wants all to come to Him."

Jake heard the people singing praise to the One in the center of it all. "Who are all these people?" Jake asked, turning toward Mic. He no longer saw him as he was. Instead, he appeared dressed in brilliant white. Adorned with powerful wings, he stood taller than before with an aura of strength and calm.

"The faithful of the ages stand before Him," Mic said. "They await the day when here will be there as well. Before that day many need to hear of the truth."

"Remember, we talked about that yesterday," Cal said. Jake looked at Cal and noticed that he and Ace appeared similar in stature with Mic, complete with wings and brilliance though not quite as tall.

"I can tell you that your father stands among them," Ace said. "All who have died believing exist in this heaven waiting for the day Jesus returns from here to there. On that day, all these will rise in glorified bodies to live there with Him. You might call that heaven 2.0. Remembering all that your parents taught you will help you find answers to your questions. And Sandy will help."

Jake wanted this feeling to go on forever. "Can I stay here?" he asked. "Better still, can I get Sandy here too?" He knew in his heart he wanted to be here.

"You only see what you have been given eyes to see," Mic said. "You only hear because you have been given ears to hear. Your time to be here is not yet. Remember this truth."

Chapter Seven

Sandy woke up to the warmth of the sun even though shaded by the trees. "Lord, thank you for an interesting day yesterday," she prayed. "Thank you for the blessings of it all, especially for Jake. The Bible he found in the emergency bag was such a gift. Please help me to show him your love and do what I can to encourage him toward you. Bless this day and all that I do, for you."

Rolling off her bed she headed to her freshening up place behind her camp. Then she headed to the beach and Jake.

— • ● • —

Jake woke up to the sound of the surf pounding the shore. He got up and visited a tree just behind the tree line. Heading back toward the beach he heard Sandy's voice calling him with an invitation for the morning swim. He met her on the beach.

"You look bright-eyed and refreshed this morning," Jake said.

"You look awake. Ready for a swim?"

"Let's go," Jake said dropping his trousers. He ran

to the water and dove in. His black nylon boxer shorts covered what needed to be covered and this way his pants wouldn't bog him down.

Sandy hit the water right behind him and side by side they swam for a while. Jake kept a watchful eye out, but so far, no sign of a shark. After a good work out, they found the sand bar from yesterday and sat on it watching the dolphins that had joined them again.

Ace made sure the dolphins kept the shark away. I bet our enjoyment of this beautiful creation delights Mic. I wonder if I should tell Sandy about my dream from last night.

"What fun to have sun, ocean and a sand bar to sit on," Jake said, watching the dolphins splashing around. "After such a great workout the growling in my stomach tells me I'm ready to get something to eat. I'll race you…" But before he could finish, Sandy dove into the water already heading to shore.

"Last one in has to do the dishes," she yelled as she swam in.

No way would Jake catch her, so he sat there and enjoyed watching her. Such a beautiful girl gliding through the water with such ease. As she got to the shallows, she walked into the shoreline wringing her long blond hair out.

She looked back at him and smiled. "Come on. Let's go to the pond and eat and then we can go to the camp and unpack the emergency bag."

Jake dove into the water and swam to the shore. Standing up, he remembered his pants and headed down the beach to retrieve them. "I'll meet you at the pond after I grab my pants."

"Alright," Sandy yelled. "See you there."

———— • ● • ————

Sandy walked to the pond. *Marooned with a good-looking guy like Jake. What a nice birthday present.*

"Lord, thanks for your gift of Jake to share this time with," she prayed. "Please give me the words to help bring him closer to you."

Nearing the pond, she picked a couple of papayas and some bread fruit. She filled the large clam shell that she kept there with fresh water and sat down on the edge of the pond to wait for Jake. She began to sing a song. "Beautiful Savior, King of creation, Son of God and Son of Man…"

———— • ● • ————

Jake heard her singing as he walked into the tree line. *I remember that beautiful song from my childhood. Sandy's voice sooths my soul.*

"Truly I'd love thee," she sang. "Truly I'd serve thee, light of my soul, my joy, my crown. Fair are the meadows, fair are the woodlands, robed in flowers of blooming spring; Jesus is fairer, Jesus is purer, He makes our sorrowing spirit sing."

"I love it," Jake said sitting down next to her. "You have a lovely voice. I remember that tune, but I didn't remember the words. Interesting."

"Here, have some fruit and a drink of water. Why did you say the words were interesting?"

"Those words tie back to a dream I've been having since I landed on the beach. I'm not sure what to make of it. Maybe you can help me understand it."

Sandy took a bite of the bread fruit followed by some water. "Tell me about your dream."

"It always starts with me floating up in the sky above myself. Three beings appear to me.   I think they might be angels from how they appeared last night. Guardian angels maybe. Not that I know what angels look like. Their names are Mic, Ace and Cal. They told me that I'm supposed to learn something from them and you so that I can see a purpose beyond this life. Twice they pointed out a shimmering wrinkle in the sky. They said Someone from there worked to bring beyond the wrinkle here. Then last night they took me through the wrinkle. It was scary amazing!"

Jake stopped. He remembered what he had seen but didn't know how to share it with Sandy.

"Don't stop now. Tell me the rest of what you dreamt."

"Beyond the wrinkle appeared a bright, white light in the center of countless people who reflected the light," Jake began. The brightness forced me to close my eyes. I couldn't look directly at it. A peaceful warmth washed over me like I've never experienced. And then I heard a voice say, 'Jake, my child, you are loved. You are mine through the water. Remember.' After that all the people began to praise the One in the center of it all. I looked up at the angel called Mic to ask who the people were. He looked different now. He appeared in brilliant white clothing. He had powerful wings and stood taller than before with an aura of strength and calm. He told me the people were the faithful of the ages waiting for the day when where we were, there, will be here as well. What does all that mean?"

"Oh my," Sandy said. "It sounds to me like you got a look at what I call heaven 1.0. When people die their physical bodies turn to dust. The soul and spirit of the faithful will be with the Lord Jesus in the heavenly realm until he returns. On that day the dead in Christ will be raised and the faithful still living will be caught up with them to meet Jesus in the sky. Heaven and earth will be changed in a flash, in the twinkling of an eye the Bible says. There will be a new heaven and new earth where all the faithful will live with Jesus forever. I call it heaven 2.0."

"One more thing," Jake said. "One of the other angels named Ace told me that my father stood among all those people. He told me to remember what my father and mother taught me and that would help answer my questions. He said you would help too. So here we are."

"What do you remember your parents teaching you? About God I mean."

"I guess you could say that they taught me by how they lived. I remember their love and kindness. They forgave me when I messed up. My dad came across tough as nails but fair. They both talked about God blessing us with so much. But I'm not sure I recognized that. I thought other people had more than us, civilians I mean. I didn't have the interaction with my dad like I did with my mom because of his constant deployments. In her easy-going way she always encouraged me to be the best I could be. I remember going to the base chapel with her as a little kid. As I got older and involved in sports my weekends mostly involved games or competitions, so I didn't go with her much. Besides, not many of my friends went to church and I noticed how

Christians acted kind of weird."

"What do you mean by weird?"

"They don't like to have fun. My parents made me tow the line, especially my dad. But I knew Christians who wouldn't let their kids dance, smoke or drink. They judge everyone and everything. Many of them pray to 'Lord Wejus,' whoever that is."

"Lord Wejus?"

"You know. 'Lord Wejus this,' or 'Lord Wejus that.'"

Sandy smiled. "You're just making fun."

"Just a little. Christians talk a lot but don't act. They don't live their lives any different from anyone else. I guess I expect Christians to be different, but I'm not sure how. They turn me off. But not you. You know about God and live what you know with happiness and joy. You, Sandy, are special."

"My parents raised me to love God and love others. I try to follow the teachings of Jesus. He gave them to us for our happiness. When people choose not to follow, they become unhappy,

unforgiving and unloving. Besides, in addition to knowing about God, I know God. That makes a difference."

Jake stood up and stretched. "We've been sitting here a while. How about we go back to camp and unpack the Christmas present? A few things in the bag will make this easy life even easier."

Jake reached down and offered Sandy a hand up. She took his hand, sending a shiver down his spine and stood looking him square in the eyes. "God wants you to know Him and have joy in Him too. No matter what happens today or tomorrow, I know God is with us surrounding us with His love."

"Ok, whatever you say," Jake said.

"Not because I say it, but because He says it. His truth you can totally rely on."

"Well, that bag at the camp holds a lot of truth we can rely on too. Let's go."

————•●•————

Jake began to unpack the survival bag. He laid out one of the space blankets and organized the items. Sandy came through the tree line with her hands behind her back. "I thought you got lost," Jake said.

"I brought us each a papaya for a snack." Sandy smiled as she handed one to Jake.

Jake bit into his, dripping juice down his chin. "Wow!" Jake said.

"I call it heavenly food like manna from heaven."

"Hey, I remember that from my Sunday school days. People in a desert wilderness needed food and God sent them manna to eat every day. But they eventually got tired of having it every day. I don't think I'll get tired of the fruit and fish here."

"God provides food for us to eat every day," Sandy said. "And remember, I'll show you where to find some clams for supper. Now, let's check out that bag."

Jake pointed to the items on the blanket. "The bag contains a handheld VHF radio and a handheld GPS. The good news is that with the GPS we can see exactly where we are. Then using the radio, we can transmit to nearby ship traffic. The bad news is that the radio needs to be within a three-to-eight-mile range of a ship. There's also flares, a signal mirror, strobes, a flashlight and extra batteries."

Jake pointed to the other side of the blanket. "On that side of the blanket I put a knife, knife sharpener, light sticks, fishing gear, waterproof matches, cordage and another space blanket. I left the trail mix, food bars, packaged water and reverse osmosis water maker in the bag. And, last but not least, a loaded first aid kit."

"Let's fire up the GPS and see where we are," Sandy suggested.

Jake shared the same thought, inserted the batteries and switched on the system. "It looks like we are way east of New Zealand and the Chatham Rise in the ocean. No land shows up immediately around us. According to the GPS we must be treading water. Bummer."

"Turn on the radio and see if anyone responds to a 'Mayday' call."

"Mayday. Mayday. If anyone hears this please respond, over." Only staticky silence came from the radio. Jake called once more. Still nothing.

"Let's put the gear away," Sandy said. "I'll show you how to dig for clams for supper. That survival knife will make opening them much easier than my smaller Swiss Army knife. Come on and I'll show you the best spot on this island for clams."

Sandy walked out along the rocky outcropping up to her knees in water. She reached down and came up with a clam. Tossing it to the beach she reached for another and tossed it as well. "Are you going to help or just stand there and watch?"

"I'm going to help," Jake answered, tossing his pants aside and walking into the surf. "I usually find them here among the rocks. Sometimes I see their air holes and dig them up. A couple of dozen ought to be plenty for our meal." She continued to toss the clams to the beach.

Jake looked in the rocks below the water line and spotted a couple and tossed them to the beach in short order. It didn't take long to have two dozen clams peppering the beach. Sandy walked back to the beach and piled their catch up.

"Jake, please take the big shell to the pond and bring it back full of water to soak the clams in. About a half hour soak will get the sand out of them. I'll get my pot and fill it with water and grab a papaya for flavor and meet you at the fire pit."

"I'll see you in a few," Jake said. He grabbed his pants and the large shell and headed for the pond. At the pond he dove in to get the salt off. *So refreshing.* Then he put his pants on. He walked to the falls and filled the shell. On his way back to camp he passed Sandy carrying a large metal pot. "Where did you find that?"

"During my first week here on one of my morning swims I noticed a reflection on the sandy bottom in about six feet of water. I went under to look and I came up with this. I have no idea where it came from."

Jake eyed the pot. *I bet Ace moved the pot from a shipwreck close enough in to shore for Sandy to see and retrieve it. Maybe he used the dolphins. He probably smiles every time she uses it.*

At the firepit Jake set the shell down and carried the clams over and put them in it. Two dozen clams filled it up. Sandy arrived with her large pot of water and a papaya and a mango.

"I use the fruit for flavor as I steam clams," she

said. "We can go back to the pond and get a couple more papaya and mangos to eat with the clams. We also need a few palm fronds to cover the pot and help steam them."

"So, how long do you have to steam the clams?" Jake asked, walking with her to the pond. "How do you know when they boil long enough?"

"Actually, when they pop open, we take them out and feast. If they don't pop, we don't eat them."

— • ● • —

Jake used one match from the emergency bag stash to start a fire. "I didn't start it with flint and steel but it will burn just the same," he said.

"When the fire burns down to a good bed of coals we can put the flat rock on them. Then we add the pot full of clams with some papaya juice in it and bring it to a boil," Sandy said. "Once it boils, we cover the top with the palm fronds to keep the steam in. We can peek in occasionally and when we see them start popping open, we take them out and dinner is served. I like to dip the meat in a little mango juice for flavor."

"Let's start with the fruit while the clams cook. I'm hungry."

"Before we eat would you mind if I offer a prayer of thanks for our food?" Sandy asked. "It might feel strange to you but God has provided this meal for us, and I think we should thank him and invite him to be with us."

"I guess that would be alright."

"Lord, thanks for this fruit and these clams, and the fresh water to go with them. You bless us by the meal and your presence."

It wasn't long and Jake noticed the clams popping open. He used a stick to pull them out setting them in the now empty large shell. Sandy showed him how she removed the meat.

After their amazing meal, they stretched back by the fire and watched the sun setting in the western sky. The coloration amazed Jake. *Such beauty!*

"Have you ever wondered how something so beautiful as this sunset could exist?" Sandy asked.

"It's just clouds and gases reflecting the sun's light."

"How did it all come together into the beautiful picture that we see?"

"It's just random happening. But you think it's a God thing, right?"

"I know that God, in His divine providence, provides this beauty to remind us of Him, to remind us of His love."

"I enjoy sitting here with you taking in the amazing view after enjoying a good meal."

The soft and warm ocean breeze along with the twilight as it gave way to the starry sky filled Jake with a similar peace to what he experienced beyond the wrinkle. *I wonder what tomorrow will bring.*

"Would you like to go exploring tomorrow after our morning swim?" Sandy asked. "I've been on this island for a year, but I've never ventured up the rock wall to the north. Now with your help and the rope from the bag we could give it a try. I've wondered what might be on the north end of this island."

"I'm up for that. Have you ever tried to swim around?'

"All the rock and rough water out from the rock wall make it appear very treacherous to me. So, no, I haven't tried."

"Let's try it after breakfast," Jake said. He got up and pulled out the VHF radio and called out another "Mayday." No response came after several attempts, so he shut it down and put it back in the bag.

"God bless you with a good night's sleep," Sandy said heading for her bed. "I'm going to call it a day. See you in the morning."

Jake took the hint, had a long drink of water from the shell and walked down the beach to his bed. He laid down and looked up at the night sky. The stars and constellations shone with brilliance. The lack of city lights made them shine even brighter. *I wonder about this Creator God that Sandy spoke of. Hard to believe that this all happened by accident without a plan.* He fell asleep with that thought.

Chapter Eight

Sandy laid on her bed prayerfully looking up at the night sky. *What a beautiful sky, Lord. Please help Jake see You in it. Use me to help him see. Send your angels to keep us safe through the night. I love You Lord.*

———•◉•———

Jake looked down at himself peacefully asleep.

"Your questions are getting answers," Mic said. "Cal, Ace and I heard Sandy talk with Him about you. She wants you to know the truth because the truth will set you free."

"What do you mean? I'm not a captive of anyone or anything."

"Yes, you are," Mic responded. "Your limited and inaccurate worldly ideas and relative perspective hold you. Free yourself by receiving the truth."

"Remember," Cal said. "Remember what He said to you."

"He said He loved me, and I became His through the water, whatever that means," Jake said. "I understand love, but what about the water stuff?"

"Do you understand God's love?" Mic asked. "He demonstrated His great love by the sacrifice of His only Son to pay the price for the sin of all. Yet, how many refuse it out of ignorance because they don't think they need it. Perhaps, even you. But a time is coming."

"What do you mean by that?"

"When the time comes, remember," Mic said.

When dawn came Jake was already awake. He started preparing for their adventure to the north side of the island. He gathered the cordage, a water bag, two energy bars, and a small, improvised version of a first aid kit into a pile. He looked down the beach and noticed Sandy get up from her bed and walk toward the trees.

"You ready for a swim and some fruit?" Jake yelled.

"Let me throw some water on my face and wake up and I'll be ready to go."

Jake's heart began to race as he watched her disappear into the trees. *I really like her.*

The sun came over the top of the trees as Sandy reappeared with a big smile on her face. "What a beautiful day the Lord made for us. I'm excited to go exploring with you later," Sandy said. Let's hit the waves and swim for a bit."

They ran into the surf and swam along the shoreline. The dolphins came alongside them again reminding Jake how Ace used the dolphins to keep them safe from anything that might harm them. *Could evil be lurking about today?*

Sandy and Jake rested by the pond as they ate fruit for breakfast. "My angels visited me again last night," Jake said. "Mic explained God's love to me like you did. He told me all about the sacrifice of His Son. He applied that to me in a cryptic way. When I asked him what he meant he said, 'When the time comes, remember.'"

"It sounds like Mic could be preparing you for something in the future. From what you told me of your parents I believe they made sure to baptize you. Because of your baptism the Spirit of God lives within you and gives you a direct connection to God the Father. Perhaps you haven't tuned in to it lately. In fact, you've probably tried to tune it out. I'll ask God to help you open yourself up to Him and help you remember."

"If you think that will help, go for it. Let's go to camp, pick up the gear I laid out and head for the north side of the island. Don't you hear it calling us?"

"Good thing we both managed to keep our tennis shoes when we arrived on the island," Sandy said. "Trying to climb up and around that rock face in bare feet would be tough. I think the rope will come in handy too."

Jake used one of the smaller bags that unzipped from the larger emergency bag for a pack and placed everything in it except for the rope. The strap from the bag went over one shoulder and the rope he put over the other. Off the two of them went north up the shoreline.

They walked by the spot where Sandy found Jake on his first day on the island. The palm blanket still lay there. A mile further and Jake heard the waves crashing on the rocks that jutted out from the shore. He faced a wall of rock. It must have been the outer wall of an old volcano rising into the sky. A mix of lava rock and stone rose up in a steep face to the rim.

Jake surveyed the wall comparing it to the rock

climbing he'd done in the past. "I think we can make an easy climb to the top. I see plenty of hand and foot holds. Between the two of us it shouldn't be too bad. Have you done any climbing?"

"Only on a smaller scale as part of a hike."

"Follow me," Jake said starting up the easiest way he could find. "The wall face goes up at about a 70-degree incline. Good news for us. I don't think we'll need the rope." Jake figured that with Sandy's athleticism she could handle the climb with ease.

Numerous places to step and hold existed close together. Only occasionally did they have to stretch a little. At those spots Jake would give Sandy an assisting hand and a gentle pull up. She climbed like a natural.

"Don't look down," Jake reminded Sandy. "Just keep focused on your current hold and your next hold and you'll be fine."

"I'm ok. I'm not afraid of heights. Climbing gets my blood moving like swimming. I'll be ready to rest when we get to the top, though."

Sitting at the top of the rim forty-five minutes later, Jake surveyed the best way down the other side. "I think we can follow the rim as it descends along this western side. It looks like a volcano that erupted and blew out the northwest side into the ocean."

"This side of the island looks as fertile as the southern only not quite as large," Sandy said. "I see the same kinds of trees, fruit trees and what looks like a pond way over there." She pointed to the northeast.

After some water and the energy bars, the pair started the descent down the rim as it curved toward the ocean. Jake noticed the footing getting damp and slippery the further down they went. A sheer wall with waves crashing below marked the ocean side. A sheer wall that dropped into lava rock with trees in the mix marked the island side.

"Take your time and be sure of your footing," Jake said. "The ocean mist and mossy surface have made this treacherous. As we get lower up ahead it looks like more sand and rock and less of this slippery stuff."

"God certainly outdid Himself with this island," Sandy said. "You have to admire the beauty of it all. He saved both of us and landed us on this tropical paradise. You must admit, it's a God thing."

"You keep telling me about that. The angels talk about it too." Jake turned with a smile just in time to see the footing under Sandy's left foot give way dropping her over the wall down into the roiling surf and rock below.

"Sandy!" Jake yelled as his eyes followed her down. He lost sight of her in the waves, trying to decide if he should risk jumping in after her. The ebb and flow of waves covered rocky outcroppings all over the place. He didn't see her anywhere.

Jake spotted a small flat just above the water line. He tied off the rope and started down. Standing on the flat, the water broke up to his knees and then down again. Sandy was nowhere to be seen. Frantic, Jake didn't know what to do. His beautiful island girl vanished.

He tightened the strap on the pack across his chest and dove in. The water took him out to sea throwing him around like a rag doll, bouncing him off the rocks but he had to search for her. At the mercy of the waves, he swam with all his might. Trying to look for Sandy and stay away from the rocks proved to be difficult.

"God, if you really are listening, please help me find Sandy. She loves You and I need her." The buoyancy of the pack at least helped to keep Jake on the surface. Out of nowhere a wave broke and smashed Jake against a massive rock and everything went black.

—•●•—

Sandy, asking for God's intervention managed to get her feet under her as she hit the water. Thankfully, the waves were coming in giving more depth. However, the force of the water pushed her into a cave or lava tube and deposited her on an interior shelf. Somehow the succeeding waves carried her through the lava tube toward an opening, continually slamming her against the walls depositing her in what appeared to be a lagoon where she came to a stop at the edge. Large strong hands pulled her out of the water, resting her on the edge of the lagoon before her senses went dark.

Chapter Nine

Jake floated in the air looking down at himself again. "You're going to be alright," he heard Mic say. "Cal made sure the dolphins pushed you out to sea and away from the danger area. They guided you toward the shore. The waves floated you to the beach."

"Forget about me," Jake said with an anger he hadn't felt since his father died. "What happened to Sandy? You said you would protect us, and you let this happen. You guys are worthless." Immediately Jake regretted saying that.

"Evil tried and once more failed against you," Mic said. "Remember the One who loves you gives you peace. As Sandy said, place your trust in Him."

"How can I trust in One I hardly know? Wait, what evil are you talking about?"

"The evil that would cause a fall," Mic said. "The evil that causes your unbridled anger against the Lord. The evil that causes you to doubt His love again."

"Remember His love and peace there," Cal said. "Remember it here, now."

"Without His love you wouldn't be here now," Ace said. "Trust that He holds you in His hands."

"How can I remember and trust in Him? In my

mind I only see Sandy falling and probably dead. It's not right."

"If it is as you say," Mic said, "She is with the Lord in heaven 1.0 as she explained to you. Do not presume to know what you do not know."

The large wave broke and rolled up on the shore covering Jake up to the shoulders waking him from his unconscious state. *That was a surprisingly hard knock on the head.* Jake got to his knees. *Interesting how I got here?* He pulled the water bag out of the pack and took a long drink. *I'm a little dehydrated.* The sun's location indicated late afternoon. Jake got to his feet and headed down the beach toward the camp. *I need to get something in my stomach.* He arrived at the spot where he first landed marked by the palm blanket and headed into the trees. *Fruit and cold water are just what I need.*

Jake approached the pond and dove in. The cool water soothed and rinsed the sand off. He got out of the pond and picked a mango and a papaya. He took the large shell and filled it with fresh water from the falls. Sitting on the edge of the pond he ate the fruit and thought about the time he and Sandy had spent there.

"This really sucks," Jake said out loud. "God, I know you are real. I saw You with my own eyes there beyond the wrinkle. I know You said you loved me. But I don't understand. Sandy told me to talk to You like I talked to my dad. Well, I need you to help me understand all this. If Sandy is somehow alive, please keep her safe and help me figure out how to find her. That's all I got for now. My head hurts and I'm hungry."

Walking through the camp he grabbed a spear and headed to the tidal pool for a couple of fish. It didn't take long before he had filets smoking over a bed of hot coals.

Chapter Ten

The frantic look in Karen Huber's eyes got Jim Evans' attention immediately. Jim, a Navy Reserve Chaplain served as the base chaplain. He also served as the pastor at a church on Oahu. He was assigned to a Reserve billet with a USMC unit at Marine Corps Base Hawaii located at Kaneohe Bay. Over the years he had been a pastor and good friend of Karen and her late husband, Stu.

Jim's years of reserve service time were front loaded with time spent on active duty in the Air Force. In addition, he had attended the Air Force Academy for a time. Karen came to see him because of their years-long friendship and his connections in the military world.

"Padre, Jake hasn't called in five days. I'm really worried. I keep trying the emergency contact number for the Legacy but I'm not getting an answer. Something's going on and I'm not sure what to do."

"You said Jake crewed on a sailboat between here and Australia," the Padre said. "Do you have any information on their sailing route or where they might be at any given time?"

"Not really. I know that they plan to be back here

in port by the end of the summer in plenty of time for Jake to begin the next school year. He called me every night or two to keep me posted on his progress. The last time he called he said he was east of New Zealand and learning a lot."

"I can check with our communications people and see if we're able to raise the boat on the ship to shore radio. I'll also speak with operations and see if we have any training flights out that way. I haven't heard of any boating emergencies in the last few days. As a crewing school trainee, Jake's probably working hard and just hasn't had a chance to call you. Let's continue praying for his safety now and for a safe return."

"Thank you, Padre. Please call me if you find out anything."

"I will be in touch no matter what," Chaplain Evans said.

— • ● • —

Jake woke up to the waves pounding the shore. Clouds rolled in from the west and a storm seemed like a real possibility later in the day. *I should check out Sandy's cave. But a morning swim would help shake the cobwebs out of my head.*

He headed into the surf. *The waves haven't been this rough since I landed on this island. I wish I had my surfboard.*

Swimming along the shore out beyond the breaking waves Jake began to think about Sandy. Her loss weighed heavily. *How can I miss her so much? I've only known her for five days. But what a great five days.*

The dolphins came by and welcomed Jake to the new day. He knew they'd saved his life the day before. *Ace said the angels watched over me. Cal said this would be a hard day and evil would try to bring me down.*

Jake staggered out of the water feeling a little dizzy. He looked to the north end of the island. *I'm going to have to go back there and complete my discovery hike of the north end. But not today.* He headed to the pond for fruit and fresh water.

He always enjoyed sitting by the pond and eating fruit. But not today. His head still ached, and he no doubt suffered from a slight concussion. His thoughts turned to Sandy and the conversations shared there at the pond.

"Lord," Jake said. "Tell me she's alright. Tell me how to find her. I know I'm kind of new at talking with You. You told me You loved me. I'll trust You to work this out for good, for both Sandy and me. And by the way, could You take away this pain in my head?"

Jake laid back and dozed off with a lingering picture of the beautiful girl God brought into his life, Sandy. The girl he prayed he hadn't lost.

Raindrops on his face brought Jake out of his sleep. He grabbed a couple mangos on his way to the camp. As he walked through the camp, he grabbed the emergency bag and headed for Sandy's cave. He found it where she said in the side of the rock wall and went inside. A six-foot round opening gave way to a fifteen-foot room before it started to narrow. Jake dug out the flashlight from the emergency bag and took a better look farther inside.

Sandy had made a bamboo and palm leaf bed. She

left a pile of tree branches for firewood and a rocked in firepit. Two large clam shells sat on a rock shelf for water. *I need to fill them before the rain gets here.* The back of the cave narrowed down until it stopped. *I think I'll stay here tonight.*

Jake made several trips to the pond for water and fruit. A light rain started to fall so he speared three fish. While he filleted them, he realized his head no longer ached.

"Lord, thanks for taking my headache away," Jake said. "Wherever Sandy finds herself, please keep her safe and dry." Back at the cave he started a fire and soon had the fillets cooking. Outside, the rain came down in sheets. The northerly wind kept it away from the cave opening. *Thanks for that too, Lord. Five days with Sandy and she rubbed off on me.*

After Jake ate the fish and some of the fruit, he threw the fruit remains and bones into the fire. Taking a drink of water, he pulled out the radio and made a Mayday call. He made several attempts, but no one responded. Just a lot of static because of the storm.

The rain continued and with the darkness of night, Jake laid on the pallet for some sleep.

It rained for two more days without letting up. Twice Jake stripped down to his boxers and went out for fish and clams and water. Without lightning or wind, the rain felt good. It was a cool shower in a warm and humid climate. Jake slept a lot during the two days. He decided that was good because of his probable concussion. Rest and sleep were the best ways to heal.

"Thank you, Lord for the healing," Jake said. He found himself talking with God more and more every day. *Why not. Sandy said He hears me and answers. He told me He loves me. Putting all of that together means conversation with Him can be constant. Since He's the only One with me, I'll talk with Him.*

Chapter Eleven

Sandy woke up to a loud crack of thunder and the pounding of rain. She opened her eyes to a bamboo roof laid with palm branches and walls also lined with bamboo poles. The air smelled of ocean breeze and storm with a hint of smoked fish. *Where am I? How did I get here?* The dim light suggested late afternoon or a heavy cloud cover. *But what day is it? How long have I been here?*

"Lord, thanks for saving me from my fall," Sandy said. "Jake must think the worst has happened. Please keep him strong and close. I know you will use this opportunity to bring him to You in some way. I'm safe in Your hands. Thanks for whoever brought me to wherever this is."

At that moment the shack door opened and a large form filled the doorway. Sandy raised her head to look but dizziness and head pain prevented it. She lapsed back into a semi-conscious state.

——— • ● • ———

"Well, little one. I see that knock on the head continues to give you grief." He dipped a cloth in cold water and laid it on her temple over the bruise. "That will help, but I need to get some water into you."

"Lord, heal her head and after she rests, wake her up to me. I can't lose my Sandy again now that You've brought her back to me."

The tsunami took David Taylor's boat and daughter a year ago and landed him on this island with a wrenched knee. Thankfully, the island supplied ample food and water. He never dreamed he would have the opportunity to save Sandy after a year. Seeing her float into the lagoon a day before the rain came, amazed and terrified him at the same time. A head injury with no medical assistance on an uninhabited island put her at the Lord's mercy. There was no one else to turn to. Even if another person could be found, David knew who would help the most and turned to the Lord.

David rinsed the cloth in the water and replaced it on Sandy's temple. Her eyelids fluttered and opened. The look of confusion in her eyes gave way to the smile he knew so well.

"Daddy, you're alive," she cried. Tears filled both their eyes at the recognition and David leaned in and hugged his daughter.

"Thank you, Lord," they said in unison.

"How long have I been out?"

"I found you in the lagoon three days ago. God floated you to me. I couldn't believe my eyes when I saw you. When I pulled you out, the lump on your forehead told me why you were unconscious. In true first aid fashion I kept a cold compress on the bruise and left the healing to the Lord."

"I've been on the other side of the island for the past year since the tsunami flipped the boat. God got me to the shore and continues to watch over me. He even sent someone a few days ago. I found a boy on the beach."

"What a nice birthday present," David said. "I've been asking God to keep you alive and safe all year. Last Sunday, on your birthday, I asked Him to give you something to keep you strong."

"His name is Jake," Sandy said. "He knows of God, but he really doesn't know God. That's been a topic of conversation between us. He can't remember what happened that he ended up in the water. He said he signed on to a sailing boat for the summer to learn how to crew. The day after I found him, we took a walk on the south end of the island. Out beyond the break water Jake noticed what turned out to be an emergency survival bag from his boat, the Legacy. It's full of helpful things, even a handheld VHS radio and a handheld GPS. The GPS indicated a position in the water east of New Zealand. According to it, no land exists anywhere around us. No one responded to our mayday call either."

"Sounds like this Jake kept you quite busy over the past week," David said. "How did you end up in the lagoon?"

"Jake and I decided to come and explore this end of the island. I didn't want to try it by myself. The climb up to the rim looked too difficult for one person. The safety factor increased with the two of us. As we started down the rim on this side, it gave way under me and caused me to fall. The sheer cliff dropped me into very rough water that swept me into a lava tube where I hit my head. I don't remember anything from then until I woke up a bit ago."

"God be praised that He brought you to me at just the right time to pull you out of the water. I'm not sure what He's up to but He's obviously up to something."

"Lord, thank you for bringing me to my dad," she prayed. "Please heal my head and give me strength so that I'm ready to be helpful to Jake. I know You are taking care of him. Use me as You wish to help him too. Thanks, Lord."

"Amen," said her dad. He could see that his daughter understood what he said by her prayer. He hoped that she understood God working in Jake's life would involve her in helping Jake understand Him.

"Now you rest for a bit and I'll get some food for you. Smoked fish and fruit are on the menu for this evening."

"Food cooked for me. That sounds great!"

— • ● • —

On day three the rain let up and the sun came out. A clear blue sky and calm water complemented the fresh smelling ocean breeze. Up with the sunrise Jake straightened the cave. He repacked the survivor bag and headed to the beach camp.

"Wow, great day God!" he said walking to the beach. *I'm going to start the day with a swim. Maybe the dolphins will be out there.*

Jake ran into the water and dove headlong into the surf. Several hundred yards out as he swam parallel to the shore, the dolphins made their appearance. *I hope Ace's vigilance against all things evil keeps it at bay.* Jake's interaction with the dolphins built his confidence about something he'd been thinking about during the rainstorm. He practiced letting them tow him around learning how to steer them where he wanted to go.

An hour later, sitting by the pond Jake ate fruit and considered his plan. "Lord, my gut tells me that Sandy didn't die in the fall. I think she's alive and somewhere on the north end of this island. Maybe that's You telling me. I don't know. But she may need my help. So, this afternoon, when the tide's out, if I can connect with the dolphins I'm going to try and swim around the rough water and onto the north end beach. Please help me do this and help me find her."

Jake ate another papaya and had a long drink of water. He went to the camp and packed the small bag with a water bottle and first aid supplies. He pulled out a knife with a case that could be strapped around his ankle. That would be good to have just in case. After attempting a mayday call with no response, he walked over to his bed and laid down for a quick nap before he attempted his swim. He dozed off with thoughts of Sandy and God and angels and dolphins.

— • ● • —

"Your fish tastes as good as mine," Sandy said with a laugh. She sat with her dad in the hut at a makeshift table he had made. "We both use the same citrus juice baste. On this island that means either mango or papaya. Yours seems to have more of a smokey taste than mine. But your grilling skill definitely beats mine when it comes to smoking fish."

"I'll take that as a compliment. But as I recall your cooking skills far out match mine thanks to your mom's efforts before she went home to be with the Lord. By the time you were nine she'd taught you all you needed to be a wiz in and out of the kitchen."

"I miss her," Sandy said. "My comfort rests in that she's with the Lord and we'll see her again in heaven or when Jesus comes back, whichever happens first."

Thoughts of her mom led Sandy to think about Jake. *I hope he found shelter from all the rain and stayed dry in my cave.*

"Dad, when my head clears I need to try and get back to Jake to let him know I'm okay, and that I found you. He'll be so surprised."

"Let's not get ahead of ourselves honey. You had a serious blow to the head. Yes, the Lord provides healing, but you need a few more days' rest before you try getting too physical. Besides, the boy you describe probably knows exactly what to do and the Lord's watching after him too."

"You're right. I'm feeling tired now, so I think I'll get some sleep."

"Good idea. I have a few things to attend to and then I'll do likewise. I love you."

"I love you too. You are such a blessing to me in so many ways. Good night, Dad."

Sandy woke up to sunlight peeking through the bamboo walls. She got up slowly to make sure of her balance and continued outside to see blue skies and smell fresh ocean air. Walking up a path she came to a lagoon. *This must be where dad found me.* The water called to her. She walked in and took a refreshing swim to the far side and back. *This feels great! I think I'll do one more lap.* Lying in bed for several days made her feel stiff but the cool water and exercise provided relief.

---•●•---

David watched Sandy enjoying the swim and knew he best not say anything more about rest. Who better to know her level of strength than her?

"You appear to be on the mend," David said. "Feeling better?"

"A lot better. But I'm not one hundred percent yet."

"After we eat, how about I show you my side of this island. An unbelievable fruit grove and waterfall wait your approval."

"That'd be great. It'll give me a chance to compare your neighborhood to mine. But I have to tell you, mine will be hard to beat. Although you do have a nice hut. The only enclosure I have, God provided in a cave within a rock wall."

David served up bread fruit, coconut and papaya on plates that looked familiar to Sandy. He served fresh water in a mug that she knew well.

"I recognize these from the boat," she said.

"Right. Fortunately, after the tsunami flipped the boat, it went down in shallow water not too far from this island. I recovered most of the gear and kitchen stuff along with clothing and such. Remember that go bag you packed? I grabbed that as well. It's in the hut under the bed. Help yourself whenever you like."

"Are you serious? You mean I have clothes and a swimming suit and toiletries?"

"Anything the salt water didn't ruin, you'll find in that bag waiting for you."

David Taylor knew fishing and boats better than

most. The sinking of his fishing boat didn't stop him from exercising a survival plan.

"I rescued some towels and other items too. The things I'm not using, I put in the little storage hut in the tree line."

"Thank you, God!" Sandy exclaimed. "This has to be the best news I've had in a year, except for Jake, and you rescuing me. God certainly used a ledge giving way and my fall for my good. Even despite a bump on the head."

———•●•———

Jake recognized himself napping below. He looked around but didn't see Mic, Cal or Ace. *I know they're here.*

"Come out, come out, wherever you are," Jake said.

At that instant Mic appeared. "Cal watched you working with the dolphins this morning.

Do you have something in mind with them?"

"I plan to let them help me swim out beyond the rough water around to the north end of the island. I'm going to look for Sandy and check out the north end."

"That will be a long swim," Cal said appearing by Mic. "The dolphins can assist you when you hit rough water or strong currents. Plus, they will help keep you safe. Evil lurks out there where you least expect it."

"I feel in my gut that Sandy is alive and somewhere on the north end," Jake said. "She may need me and I'm not going to let her down. I've asked the Lord to help me. I know He will."

"Do you know the Lord's will?" Mic asked. "The

events of life can be difficult to understand. He wants you to live in tune with His will. He desires all too. The best way to get it right involves talking with Him about it. Always remember to ask for His will to be done for Him, not for you. That will be best for you."

"You know you often talk in riddles," Jake said. "I'm beginning to understand a bigger picture here. I still have a few questions that I want to kick around with Sandy. So, you three will need to be on high alert this afternoon."

"We always stand ready to assist you," Ace said. "Only remember we serve Him in serving you."

Jake strapped the knife around his ankle and the bag around his chest and dove into the surf. The cool water and light breeze invigorated him. The waterproof bag around his chest provided for some floatation. Jake swam about a half mile out from shore picking up the dolphins along the way. *I'll have to thank Cal for your help.*

As Jake turned north and the dolphins turned with him, he prayed, "Lord, please keep the sharks away and anything else that might get in the way as I circle around the island."

I know He hears me. I just hope I'm doing what He wants. I know it's what I want.

Jake swam for about a mile by his calculations and then he turned east. He made unimpeded progress toward reaching the north shore until a notched dorsal fin rose out of the water. *There he is again. Always lurking around. I've got a pod of dolphins and a knife. But I've also got the Lord with me. Not going to worry. I bet that makes Cal smile. I can hear him tell the others, 'He's getting it.' Then Mic will come up with something cryptic like, "The evil lurks but we keep it at bay."*

Jake swam the third leg into the beach. *What a workout. It feels good though.*

"Thanks Lord, for getting me here," Jake said. He looked around and noticed the similarity to the south side of the island. *It ought to be. It's the same island.*

A tree line ran along the island side of the beach like at Sandy's camp. He walked into it and found a worn path. *Somebody's been here.* Through the trees he walked into a clearing with a bamboo hut in the middle of it.

"Lord, I don't think Sandy's had time to build something like that," he said. His neck hair bristled at the thought. *There's someone else here.*

He walked toward the hut and noticed a smaller one at the back tree line. No one appeared to be around. Using the defensive training he learned with the marines, he scouted the perimeter of the clearing. He noted the lagoon beyond the clearing. Still not seeing anyone, he went back to explore the hut.

Inside, a bed and a table with metal dishware took up most of the space. *Interesting.* On the bed, something even more interesting caught his eye. Sandy's shorts and top next to a bag of clothes and things. *She's been here. She's alive.*

He ran out the door and came face to face with a big guy at six foot six. Jake wasn't quite sure what to make of him. He had broad shoulders and big hands and stood solid as a rock.

"I'm going to make an educated guess that you're Jake," David said with a smile. "Welcome to the north side of the island. My name is David. I'm Sandy's dad.

I just returned from a hike with Sandy."

With excitement growing inside Jake asked, "You've been here for a year and didn't know about Sandy on the south side of the island?"

"I messed up my knee when the boat flipped," David said. "I stayed with it until it sank in the shallows out a ways north from here. With a life jacket I ferried a lot of gear from the wreck to this beach. My wobbly knee prevented me from trying to trek over the volcano wall and explore south of here. I didn't know if Sandy survived or not. I left her in the Lord's hands. What a surprise when she floated into the lagoon a few days ago."

"So, she's here," Jake said with an excitement he could hardly contain. "Where? I've got to see her."

"We took a walk to a grove of fruit trees with a waterfall nearby. She wanted to stay there and talk with the Lord for a while. I'm thinking that conversation involved you."

"What direction do I go?" Jake asked.

"Follow that path over there to the east for a half mile or so and you will find it and her. I'll have something ready for supper when you get back."

Before David could finish the sentence, Jake headed off to the east through the trees to the girl that he desperately needed to see.

Jake heard the waterfall crashing over the rocks and into the pond below it. The sound came from beyond a small rise. He came over the rise into a grove of fruit trees remarkably similar to the trees on the south end of the island. Full of fruit, they beckoned pickers.

Not interested in eating at the moment, Jake

scanned the area for Sandy. *Come on. Where could she be?* He double checked the pond. No Sandy swimming in it. Coming up empty he headed back toward David's camp.

"Lord, thanks for keeping her alive and safe," Jake said moving through the trees. The smell of the warm earthy air reminded him of the forests on Oahu. "You kept me safe back home when I got lost. Now, You've kept Sandy safe when she fell over the cliff, lost to me. I'm glad I finally got to know You."

"You have?"

Jake wheeled around and there stood Sandy three feet away leaning against a tree looking as beautiful as ever. He ran up to her and gave her a hug that said, "I'm never letting you go." Sandy hugged back with a tear in her eye.

"How did you find me?"

"It's what you call a God thing," Jake said with a laugh.

Chapter Twelve

"Karen, I've got some news," Padre Evans said reassuringly. He called Jake's mom after hearing from the command chaplain of the 1st Marine Aircraft Wing stationed at Iwakuni, Japan. He'd put a call in to his longtime friend a few days earlier asking about information on a boat called the Legacy sailing east of New Zealand.

"Some kind of incident happened on the Legacy during a nighttime storm that resulted in two boys going overboard," Chaplain Dunn told me. "The crew tossed one of the emergency packs into the water hoping it would float in the same vicinity as the boys and render some help. The Legacy crew recovered one of the boys. The search continues for the other boy. No names have been released yet. During the incident the Legacy's radio quit working for some reason. Once repaired, the Captain of the Legacy reached out to the Australian Maritime Coast Guard, the Royal Australian Navy, the United States Coast Guard, and the United States Navy for assistance with the search."

Padre Evans continued, "When the USMC heard the word and that we were concerned about MSgt. Huber's son Jake, they immediately ramped up air recon efforts. They redirected several training flights in the direction of the Legacy. Marines always take care of their own and you and Jake are part of the family."

"Thank you, Padre," Karen said. "I haven't heard anything from the Legacy people yet. Why haven't they told me if Jake's the missing boy, I'm so worried. I feel helpless to do anything."

"Karen, just keep talking with the Lord and give your worry over to Him. I'll stop by later today to check in on you."

"Thank you again, Padre."

"No better place exists for Jake or any of us than being in the Lord's hands. Besides, Jake has a lot of survival training under his belt. Stu and Jake's Marine friends have seen to that. If anyone can survive a difficult situation, he can. But as you said we don't even know if Jake's the one missing."

———•●•———

"I bet that iridescent green swimsuit glows in the dark," Jake said as he loosened his embrace. "It looks great, especially on you. I can't believe I missed you when I walked by before."

"I was sitting over behind those trees talking with the Lord when I heard you walk by. You looked like a guy on a mission, so I thought I'd wait here for your return. I knew you'd have to come back by here."

"When you fell, I thought you were a goner," Jake said. "I climbed over the side and down to water level searching for you. I dove in to search, using the pack for flotation, but the rough water threw me around like a rag doll. I ended up smacking my head on the rocks and the current pulled me out to sea. I woke up on the beach a little north of your camp. I'm certain that Mic, Cal, Ace and the dolphins share responsibility for that."

"Sounds like a God thing to me. He's been looking out for you your whole life. I think He's got a plan for you that's starting to unfold now."

"I think you may be right. I just wish His plan didn't come with so much pain attached. When I woke up on the beach, I had a headache that wouldn't quit. The rock wall my head hit no doubt gave me a slight concussion. Your fall and loss made me so angry I didn't think to ask for God's help until the next day. I'm thankful He provided healing for my head pain."

"He healed us both from head injuries. When I fell, the waves pushed me into an old lava tube and I smacked my head on the wall. I believe God got me through the tube and into the lagoon where my dad found me. He said I lay unconscious for a day. Several days passed before my head cleared. Today is the best I've felt since I fell. Although, when I came to and looked into my dad's eyes looking back at me, I couldn't thank God enough."

"I ran into your dad at the hut, literally," Jake said. "I swam around to this end of the island with a dolphin assist. I walked up the beach and into the tree line and came through by the hut. I didn't see anyone, so I went inside to look around. Your clothes on the bed got my blood moving. I ran out to look for you and ran right into your dad. He's a big man! What is he about six foot six and two hundred and forty pounds?"

"Yep, that's my dad."

"After he introduced himself, he pointed this way and said I'd find you here by the pond. Thank God I found you alive and safe. We've only known each other for a few days but I missed you. Every day I thought about you, things you said and did. I stayed in your rock cave during the storm. Everything I did for water and food matched what you had done, like the clam shell for water storage. You laid the place out perfectly with the bed in good shape too."

"I missed you too. I knew you could take care of yourself but I didn't know how you'd react thinking I had drowned or something. I'm glad you liked the cave. I hadn't been in it for a while so it might have been a bit of a mess."

"Let's head back to the camp. Your dad said he would get supper ready and I really am hungry."

— • ● • —

"What a great meal, sir," Jake said. "Especially since you did all the work."

"Not all the work," David said. "The Lord provided it all for us. I just put it together and smoked the fish for that outback taste. There's not much a person can do to improve on the taste of papaya and mango."

"Good cooks run in my family," Sandy said. "Mom taught us both. She was a great chef and teacher."

"Actually, she taught you and you taught me when you came fishing with me," David said. "My cooking results from your mom's influence through you sweetie."

"Between the two of you, I've learned more about cooking over the past week and a half than my entire life," Jake said. "That includes what I learned during survival training. I don't think I ever stayed home long enough to learn from my mom. I've been blessed. Oh, did I just say that?"

"Yes, you did," Sandy said. "I'm glad to hear you say it. Your blessing comes from God who you're starting to know in your heart. The more you recognize that, the closer you are to Him. Whatever He has in store for you depends on that closeness."

"Well, I see that this conversation began long before you two arrived here at my camp," David said.

"Yes sir, it did," Jake said. "Once Sandy discovered that I knew a little about God, but that I really didn't know Him she began to enlighten me. My knowledge of God continues to grow because of her and the three angels I've been seeing."

"Three angels," David said. "Tell me about them."

"I first encountered them after I ended up on the beach," Jake said. "They go by Mic, Cal and Ace. But I've since found out that their full names are Michael, Caleb and Grace. I learned that when they took me through the wrinkle to see all the saints gathered around the throne and Jesus. The three appeared larger than life, brilliant white wings and all. The biggest thing was that I heard Jesus tell me I belonged to Him through the water."

"Dad, close your mouth," Sandy said. "Jake's visions with the angels have continued ever since he got here. He shares them with me so that I can help him understand them. Everything he sees and hears I know from the Bible. His experience strengthens my faith."

"That's amazing," David said. "God's doing something here with all of us. While it strengthens our faith in what we know and believe, it could also be challenging to us. We need to be ready for whatever that is."

"That sounds ominous," Jake said.

"We face challenges here every day and the Lord protects us. We have nothing to fear with Him by our side. Well, it's getting late. I'll clean up from supper. Why don't the two of you take a walk on the beach and watch the sun set."

"I'd like that," Sandy said. "How about it, Jake?"

"Let's go."

Sandy and Jake walked the beach for a while. Jake wanted to take hold of Sandy's hand as they walked and asked, "Ok if I hold your hand?"

"I'd like that," Sandy said.

Touching her sent shivers up Jake's arm.

"Finding your dad alive and joining him on this end of the island gave me an idea. What do you think about staying here with him?"

"It would be better to stay here with him than try and get him over the rim or around in the water to the other side. What about the emergency bag equipment? We could use that here."

"I thought about that," Jake said. "In place of my morning swim how about if I swim around, get a bite and rest up for a couple of hours, and then swim back using the emergency bag for a raft. Piece of cake. Especially if the dolphins lend a fin."

"Very funny. Let's talk with God about it and decide in the morning," she said, as she squeezed Jake's hand. "For now, let's walk back toward the camp and sit and watch the sun go down on a beautiful day the Lord made for us."

Sitting on the beach, they watched the pink and red and orange sunset. *What a remarkable sight.* "I don't think I will ever tire of seeing that," Jake said. "While aboard the Legacy, we watched it every evening. I wonder about the crew. Could they still be looking for me?"

"I pray for that every day," Sandy said. "That highlights the importance of getting the radio. We might be able to contact them, or someone to rescue us. Not that we find ourselves in any harm or danger here. God has blessed us with each other and everything else we need to survive."

Jake leaned against her shoulder and listened to the waves crash against the shore as the sun went down. *Lord, I'm glad for all that Sandy does to help me get to know You better.*

Jake felt Sandy next to him and realized he still held her hand. *I'm on a beach in the south pacific with a great girl watching the sunset. I couldn't be more blessed.*

"Hey, you two," they heard David yell. "Before it gets dark, we have to get something together for Jake to sleep on in the hut so the mosquitoes don't eat him alive."

Sandy and Jake looked at each other and smiled. Jake could picture the smile on Ace's face. He was doing his thing keeping the mosquitoes away.

"Mosquitoes stay away from us," Sandy told her dad as she and Jake returned to the camp. "I'm sure it's a God thing."

Jake wiped the sweat from his forehead. "We can cobble together a bamboo frame up off the ground and use palm branches and leaves across it. I'll be fine out here."

"In that case you can use the bed I made when I first arrived on the island," David said. "You'll find it over there by the trail into the camp. We can freshen it up and you'll sleep like a baby."

All three went to work gathering palm leaves.

"That looks ship shape," Jake said standing back and admiring the cushy platform.

"Let's go sit by the fire for a while," Sandy said. "We can share with dad our thoughts for tomorrow. And we can ask for the Lord's blessing on what we want to do."

———•●•———

"I enjoy sitting here by the fire with the two of you," Jake said. "I miss my mom and dad, especially my dad, but sitting here with you feels like family."

"The Lord always provides for our needs," David said. "In this case, you for us and we for you. I think He brought you here to bring you closer to Himself. Also, because of your being here, Sandy and I found each other."

"I have to admit sir, meeting and getting to know your daughter changed my life. I think she's the smartest, bravest, best-looking girl in the world. On top of that, she helped me get to know the Lord personally. She will always be on my mind and I hope in my life."

"The Lord brought us together," Sandy said. "I'm sure of that. I like having you around too. I'll leave it to the Lord to keep you safe if He leads you to decide to swim around to our old camp in the morning. In fact, I'll swim the first leg out with you. I can use the exercise."

"I'll keep you both in my prayers tonight," David said. "Both of you are strong willed. I'll pray that you'll tune in to the Lord and let Him guide you into His future for you."

With stiff muscles and a yawn Jake said, "I'm gonna hit the rack. See you both in the morning."

"God bless you with a good night's rest," Sandy said.

Jake caught her watching him out of the side of his eye. Before he reached the trees he turned and smiled and said, "God bless you too."

Jake stretched out on the palm leaf bed thinking about how great the day had been. *Lord, what are You up to? Should I make the swim tomorrow and bring the emergency gear back here or do You have something else in mind? I'm not sure how to figure out what You want. This is kind of new for me. I know You're there. I know You hear. Please let me know.* He yawned and went to sleep.

"Hey Mic," Jake said looking down on himself asleep as the angel floated next to him. "You could have told me Sandy found her father, or that her father found her alive."

"Sandy will live forever in the Lord," Mic said. "The passion in your soul drives you. In our Lord, that is a good thing. He uses passion to empower people for His glory. But always in His love."

"Umm, could you be a little less cryptic?"

"You have received insights experienced by only a few. Sandy, and now her father, help you to put those insights into use for the Lord. Consider your entire life until now a learning experience. Very soon you will be challenged by the evil lurking around. Always remember He loves you. Trust in that love. Trust Him. Sleep now. Tomorrow, you have a long swim."

Chapter Thirteen

Jake woke to the surf pounding on the shore. He got up and found Sandy sitting across from him, staring at him.

"What?" Jake asked.

"I woke up, so I thought I'd come here to welcome the day with you. You were sleeping so soundly I didn't want to wake you. Besides, I kinda like having you around."

"The feeling's mutual."

"You've got a big day in front of you if you plan to swim around to our old camp and back again. I thought a light breakfast of fruit would be in order. Back at the camp I have some mangos and papayas and bananas."

"Let's go eat and get this show on the road."

"I'm amazed that the mosquitoes didn't dine on you last night," David said as they sat at the camp. "It is truly a God thing. I've been battling them for a year since I arrived here. But Sandy says you've had no problems with them. I thought mosquitos only inhabited this north side of the island. But apparently not."

"Enough chit chat you two," Sandy said. "The surf's choppy this morning and clouds are rolling around like there could be a storm brewing. So, let's eat and get going."

After eating, Jake double-checked the watertightness of the bag he'd brought with him. Satisfied, he picked it up and the three of them walked to the beach.

"Dad, since I'm not one hundred percent, I'm only going to swim the first leg with Jake," Sandy said, "and then I'll swim back. That's about one third of the way for him and I need the exercise."

Jake walked over to David and shook his hand goodbye. David grabbed his hand, pulled him in for a fatherly hug. "The Lord go with you and bring you safely back again."

David's hug reminded Jake of his father's. The soothing nature of it lowered his anxiety and stress. He turned to Sandy.

"Anything I can bring back for you besides the emergency bag?" he asked.

"Just yourself please," Sandy said. Jake could see the concern in her eyes. He knew she didn't want him to go but that they needed him to.

"Oh, and we don't have anything here like my cooking pot. If you can, please bring it."

She leaned in and hugged him. Her warmth and strength energized him. He realized the special nature of her relationship with him. The sense that all would be well filled Jake.

"Ok," Jake said. "We'll swim out northwest a ways and then I'll turn west and you come back here. That's the plan, right? But if you start to tire, you turn back. Got it?"

"I'll be fine," Sandy said. "I can use a little more challenging exercise."

Jake took off his pants and dropped them on the beach, intending to swim in his shorts. "I'll leave these here till I get back this evening." He picked up the small waterproof bag and put the strap over his shoulder. Grabbing Sandy's hand he said, "Let's go." Into the surf they went.

They arrived at the point that Jake was ready to turn west. The clouds building in the east and the five-foot swells indicated a storm on the way.

"Time for you to turn back," Jake said treading water with the assist from the bag. "Here, hold on to me and rest for a minute," he said, bringing Sandy in close.

"It feels good to be swimming out here," Sandy said. "Especially with you."

She looked strong Jake thought, so no problem swimming back to shore.

Sandy looked deeply into his eyes and smiled. "You be safe and we'll see you this evening." She hugged him and lightly kissed him on the cheek. "I pray the Lord will go with you and keep you strong."

He looked her in the eyes and said, "The Lord be with you too."

He didn't fully understand the power of the prayers he and Sandy and David lifted to the Lord. He knew time would tell.

The surf continued building and the clouds continued moving in. *I hope Sandy doesn't get caught in a rip tide before she reaches the shore.* Eyeing the ominous weather, he lifted Sandy up before the Lord.

Jake found himself on the edge of the island's rough water, only he appeared to be further west of the island than when he first swam around. The current carried him further from the island than he intended to be.

"What's going on, Lord?" Jake asked as the water pulled him further west. *Where are the dolphins?*

He continued swimming south but ended up further and further west of the island. Only then did he realize the rip tide and the current carrying him west away from the island.

Jake tried to swim southeast against the current for the better part of an hour but made no progress. In fact, the island got smaller and smaller. *Not good.*

Jake tightened the strap of the bag around himself, put his arms around it, and rested.

"Lord, I need your help here," Jake said floating away from the island. "I trust You, but I'm wearing out from the roughness of this water."

Jake put his head on the bag and held on for hours half asleep and half awake. The roiling surf of the storm continued to batter him. As the island disappeared from sight Jake remembered where he had been ten days earlier. Right here.

— • ● • —

"You've been here before," Mic said as he and Jake looked down on Jake unconsciously afloat in the water.

"What's going on?" Jake asked. "I planned on the Lord helping me get around the island and then back to Sandy and her dad."

"Often God's will doesn't align with what a person thinks or wants. Remember, He wants only good for those He loves. He loves you and His goodness revolves around His purpose for you."

"He has a funny way of showing it. If getting carried so far east that I can't see the island aligns with His purpose, I don't understand. I wanted to help Sandy and her dad. By getting the emergency bag and getting back to them, I could help get us all rescued."

"All power and all knowledge reside in our Lord. Rescue will happen in His time as He wills it. Until then you have a purpose higher than rescue. The evil that gets in the way challenges you to overcome according to your love and trust of Him."

"What evil are you talking about?"

"The evil that causes rough surf and rip tides to spoil your plans. The evil that has you holding on to a bag in the ocean instead of back at your camp. The evil that causes thoughts of the Lord's indifference toward you when in fact He loves you. This evil challenges your faith."

"You did tell me about a challenge," Jake remembered.

"Even in the face of this evil, some has been kept at bay. Cal and Ace have been protecting you from several of Luce's physical trials. He desires to bring you down any way he can. His power and shrewdness can overwhelm but because of the One, you have won."

"There you go getting cryptic again."

"Then let's get real, Jake," Mic said. "This world is full of evil because of Luce. Jesus is the One who beat him down by dying. Not for himself. He was perfect. He died for you and all who need a way back to the Lord. His death is yours. He rose from death to life leading the way for you and all. You receive it by believing in Him. Luce wants to keep as many from that belief as possible. When Jesus brings there to here only those who believe in Him will be with Him here forever. Got it?"

— • ● • —

"Hey Padre!" Captain Hardy the Commanding Officer of the USS Theodore Roosevelt, CVN 71, an aircraft carrier in the western Pacific yelled to Chaplain Evans standing on the signal bridge. "One of our Seahawks spotted something afloat in the search grid. The report told of something or someone in the water."

Chaplain Evans had boarded the carrier earlier in the week by a COD (carrier onboard delivery) flight from Okinawa, Japan. The Marines on board comprised part of the command he served at MCB Hawaii located at Kaneohe, Oahu. Aboard to inspect the Command Religious Program of the USMC unit, Chaplain Evans advocated for search and rescue operations in the area where a faint Mayday call had been received days earlier.

"Captain, will the Seahawk crew be able to make a rescue?" Chaplain Evans asked.

"Rough seas from the storm that went through continue. The Seahawk will stay on station anticipating that as the storm passes, the surf will calm enough for them to make an extraction. It could be upwards of an hour before we know anything more."

"A small chance exists it could be Jake Huber," Chaplain Evans said.

"Padre, I know you're a man of prayer so why don't you make yourself comfortable in my at-sea cabin and do your thing. I'll keep you posted if we hear anything more."

"Skipper, if it's all the same to you, I'd like to stay out here on the signal bridge. I like the fresh air, the view, and the conversation with the Lord has been ongoing for a while now."

"Copy that."

——————•●•——————

The sea is calm enough for us to attempt a rescue," Chief Dave Jones, the crew chief, said to the pilot of the Seahawk. "Petty Officer Corkeron will let me down on the tether and I will put the harness on the kid and we'll both come up together. Piece of cake."

"I like your confidence," LT Foley, the pilot, said. "But let's not take any chances. Do it safe and by the book."

"Copy that. The kid's been in the water for ten days. He's got part of an emergency bag strapped around himself. So, maybe he had access to the full bag. But I don't know how he's still alive. We need to get him up, ASAP."

"Copy that," LT Foley said. "Execute the rescue now."

"I'm away," the Chief said over the intercom indicating he hung by the line free of the Sea Hawk. "Hold her steady here Skipper and PO3 Corkeron will put me right on top of him."

"Copy that." LT Foley said.

PO3 Corkeron lowered the Chief down into the water right next to Jake. The Chief checked Jake for a pulse and found one beating strong. When the Chief put his hand on Jake's neck he opened his eyes.

"You Jake Huber?"

"Yeah," Jake croaked. The Chief figured his throat was parched from salt water.

"He's alive," the Chief radioed. "He said he's Jake Huber."

"Copy that," LT Foley said. "Get the harness around him and get him aboard."

"How did you find me?" Jake asked while the Chief wrapped the harness around his upper body. "I've only been floating out here for a day."

"Never mind that now. Let's get you into this harness and up into the chopper. By the way, you went overboard off the Legacy ten days ago."

The Chief gave a thumbs up and the winch started to bring them up.

"We're both aboard skipper," the Chief said. "Let's head for the ship."

"Wait," Jake yelled. "Two more people need to be rescued. On the island just east of here."

"Maybe you imagined them," the Chief said laughing it off. "You're probably delirious from being adrift in the water for ten days."

"No, I'm serious," Jake said. "I spent most of the last ten days you mentioned with two other people stranded on an island. A tsunami shipwrecked David and Sandy Taylor there about a year ago."

"What are you talking about? No island shows up east of here. At least not on any maps I've seen. Hold on."

"Skipper," the chief said. "For the record, the kid says there are two more needing rescue on some island east of here. I don't know how accurate that is. He's been in the water for ten days. I thought you should know what he said."

"Copy that," LT Foley said. "We've still got fuel to burn so I'll make a swing to the east and see if we pick up anything."

—•●•—

"Padre," Captain Hardy said, coming through the hatch to the signal bridge. "The pilot of the Seahawk just radioed that they picked up Jake Huber from the water. I am amazed he's still alive. We're notifying the Legacy and other search teams. One hiccup presented itself though. The kid says two more people need rescue on an island east of where they picked him up. He says he spent most of the ten days he was missing on the island. The fact that no islands show up on the map of that area causes a problem."

"I've known Jake his whole life," Chaplain Evans said. "He's a straight shooter and a good kid. He wouldn't make something like that up."

"The crew chief of the Seahawk thinks he may be a little delirious from being in the water for ten days. The pilot said he would search to the east of the rescue position until his fuel dictated a return to the ship."

"If you don't mind, Skipper, I'd like to radio MCB Hawaii and have them contact Jake's mom. She's been worried sick about him, and I told her if I learned anything during my inspection out here, I'd let her know."

"Sure, Padre, go ahead. Extend my greetings to Mrs. Huber as well. In the meantime, I'll have the command do a search for the people Jake said he shared the island with to see what they can find. When the Seahawk returns and Jake's been through medical we can pursue it further."

"Aye aye, Sir."

———•●•———

Aboard the Seahawk Jake took a long pull on the water bottle. The cold water revived him and helped to clear his head. He determined to add his eyes to the crew's as they searched for the island he'd spent the last ten days on.

"The skipper says he's been flying due east since we picked you up but there's no island in sight," the Chief said. "Just a lot of ocean. We're going to have to turn back to the ship because our fuel level demands it. Are you sure you didn't just dream this island thing up because you didn't have food or water for ten days and suffered from delirium?"

"Come on, Chief, how could I be in such good shape if I've been floating for ten days without food or water? You think I just dreamt up an island and a couple of people shipwrecked there?"

"Kid, I've heard stranger things from people adrift for less than ten days. For now, just lay back and relax. We'll be aboard the Roosevelt in no time. They'll run you through medical to make sure you're ok. Then you'll be able to debrief with the XO. You can tell him about the past ten days and your island and he'll decide next steps."

Jake laid back and relaxed. *How did I float so far from the island? The storm and the rip tide must have taken me. Lord, this is nuts. I know the island is there. I know Sandy and her dad are there. Help me figure out how to find them.*

Jake's exhaustion finally caught up with him and the engine of the Seahawk with its accompanying vibration rocked Jake to sleep within minutes. Floating for hours and battling the rough surf had taken a physical toll and sleep came fast.

Chapter Fourteen

Karen answered the door to find Religious Program Specialist 1st Class Justin Owens standing in front of her with a big smile on his face.

"Good morning, Mrs. Huber," RP1 Owens said. "May I come in?"

"Yes, come in."

"Mam, we received word from Chaplain Evans, who is aboard the Roosevelt, that they found and rescued your son Jake. He's alive and well. Captain Harding sends his regards."

Tears of joy rolled down Karen's cheeks. "God be praised, my Jake's alive. Where did they find him?"

"The crew of a Seahawk off the Roosevelt spotted him floating in the search grid way east of New Zealand. A faint distress signal heard a few days ago reoriented the search. The crew rescued him. That's all I know right now."

"What happens next?"

"The medical team will give Jake a thorough exam and make sure he's ok. After that, the Command will debrief him and he'll no doubt contact you. If I hear anything more, I'll let you know asap."

"I am so happy. You really made my day."

"Yes Mam. It's a great day in the Lord."

———•●•———

"Hey Padre," Jake said. "It's been a while."

"Hi Jake," Chaplain Evans said, entering the sickbay room. "How are you feeling this morning? The Doc says you're in great shape for someone who spent ten days adrift in the ocean without food and fresh water."

"I feel great. But I need someone to believe me. I only spent a day in the water. The nine days before that I was on an island with two others, David Taylor and his daughter Sandy. They became shipwrecked on the island about a year ago. A tsunami swamped their fishing boat and it sank not too far from the island where we found each other."

"Are you sure you didn't dream it, Jake?"

"Padre, like I told the XO, how could a dream keep me as healthy and well-fed as I am? Besides, I know the difference between a dream and reality. I didn't tell the XO about the dream or vision that I did have. I've been saving that conversation for you."

"Go ahead. I'm listening."

"You're going to think I'm nuts, Padre."

"Let me be the judge of that. Tell me."

"It all started with me up in the air looking down on my body lying on the beach of an island. An angel named Mic started talking with me and before I knew it Cal and Ace, two more angels, appeared on either side of me. They told me He sent them to keep me safe and help me learn about Him so that I would in some way help others know about Him. In a later vision, I learned that He was the Creator God, and His Son is Jesus. He also told me that He loved me and I belonged to Him through the water."

"Wow. What do you think about that?"

"Well, I had several more encounters or visions after that first one over the nine days I stayed on the island. Sandy Taylor, the girl that found me on the beach, turned out to be the first true example of a Christian my age I've met. She helped me understand what the angels told me. In fact, Mic told me she would help me understand it all."

"The first angel you saw, you called Mic, right?"

"Yes. I found out in a later vision the reality of his full identity, Michael the Archangel. I actually witnessed the throne with Jesus and the throng of believers all dressed in white."

"Wait. You're telling me you saw heaven?"

"Actually, as Sandy helped me understand, it's what she calls heaven 1.0. Where all the believers in Christ who have died reside with Him until He returns and the resurrection happens and believers live with Him on the new earth, heaven 2.0."

"That's amazing, Jake," Chaplain Evans said. "So, two people out there still need rescue."

"I've been trying to tell everyone that. But they all say I must have been dreaming, or delirious or something."

"What an amazing story Jake. But I believe you. I'll make sure the Captain hears about it too. The big question to be answered involves the location of the island. Nothing shows up on the map."

"It should be east of where the Seahawk picked me up. How far I really don't know."

"I'll encourage the Captain to keep looking. In the meantime, I thought you might like to call your mom. I heard the worry in her voice when she told me you didn't phone her early on. I sent word of your rescue, and I know she'd like to hear from you. I set it up with communications. You can call from that phone next to your bed. Just pick up and tell the operator and they'll put it through."

"Thanks, Padre. You're the best."

The chaplain walked out the door and Jake grabbed the phone. While he waited for his mom to answer, he thought about Sandy and her dad. *They must wonder what happened to me. Lord, please keep them safe and help them not to worry too much about me.*

"Hello, Jake?"

"Hey Mom."

"Oh Jake, I was so worried about you," Karen said. "When you didn't call after a couple of days, I knew something happened to you"

"It's okay, Mom. I'm fine. I spent a day in the water. Other than that, I couldn't be better. I spent nine days on an island with a girl named Sandy and her father David. They'd been ship-wrecked on the island for a year. It was a God-thing that I ended up being rescued by the Seahawk crew. Hopefully, they will be able to find the island and rescue them too."

"Honey, I'm so glad they found you. I'm not sure I could handle losing you too."

"Mom, it's cool. The Lord took care of me."

"You've mentioned 'the Lord' a second time. What's up with that? Not that I'm complaining."

"I have a new appreciation for being connected to God through Jesus. My experience on the island reminded me how much He loves me. Sandy, the girl shipwrecked there, helped me understand in a way that I never had before. I'll explain more when my crew training is finished and I get back home. I'm going to stay on the Roosevelt for a few days to try and help them find the island and rescue the Taylors. Then I want to get back on the Legacy and finish my summer training."

"Oh, I don't know Jake. I think I want you home."

"Mom, you know what dad would say."

"I know. I know. He'd say, 'Adapt and overcome.' But you're only 16 and you've been through so much."

"I love you, Mom. But dad taught me how to handle myself in situations like this. Besides, the Lord has bigger things in store for me. I have a new appreciation for being connected to God through Jesus. My experience on the island reminded me how much He loves me. Sandy, the girl shipwrecked there helped me understand in a way that I never had before. I'll explain more when my crew training is finished and I get back home. In the meantime, keep praying for me and for the Taylors that the Lord would help us find and rescue them."

"Oh, Jake. Now I have so many questions."

"I know, Mom. Chaplain Evans will probably get back there before I do so he can answer some of them. I'm good, Mom. I love you."

"I love you too, Jake. Please be careful and come home safe. I pray for you every day."

———•●•———

"I don't understand why Jake didn't come back

yesterday," Sandy said.

Sitting around the morning campfire wondering what might have happened to him was no fun.

"The swim around must have been tougher than either of you thought it would be," David said. "The weather change and the riptide certainly played into it. I'm sure Jake decided to rest up before he tried the return swim. Let's pray that he's safe and see what today brings."

"I've been talking with the Lord about Jake since yesterday evening," Sandy said. "I hope he gets back soon."

Sandy couldn't shake Jake's safety from her mind. That was bad enough. She considered the treacherous swim around to her camp or climbing the volcanic rim that had almost killed her the first time. She cringed at either option. Neither was a good idea to her.

Chapter Fifteen

Jake heard the rap on the door frame. He looked up into the eyes of a Navy petty officer looking sharp and standing tall with a security band on her sleeve.

"Hi Jake," said Petty Officer 2nd Class Anna Rodriguez. "The XO would like a word with you. He asked me to escort you up to the bridge. He thought you might like to get out of this room for a bit and stretch your legs."

"Petty Officer Rodriguez, that would be great," Jake said.

"Please, call me Anna," the Petty Officer said. "If you'll follow me, I'll show you the way. We will be going several decks up and forward from sickbay to the bridge."

"Lead the way."

He followed Anna along passageways and up ladders until they got to the flight deck level. The cleaning crew, mopping and waxing, blocked the ladder up to the bridge, so they needed to go up the starboard side ladder.

"The shortest way to the starboard ladder is to go out this hatch to the flight deck, walk around the tower, and enter on the other side," Anna said. "Stay right behind me and you'll be fine."

"I'm on your six," Jake said.

They proceeded around a blackout wall under red lighting and stepped out onto the flight deck. Eerily dark with no flight ops happening, Jake couldn't see his hand in front of his face.

After ten or twelve steps into the dark unknown Jake lost Anna. He took two steps to the side feeling out with his hands hoping to touch the tower wall but grabbed a handful of air.

"Anna," Jake called out, trying to stay calm but at the same time terrified he would walk over the side and end up in the water, again. *Lord, I'm in your hands.*

"Anna," Jake called out louder than before.

"Jake, where are you?" Anna called out.

"I'm here. Keep talking and I'll come to your voice."

"Be careful of the tie downs on the deck. Slowly walk toward my voice."

Jake had his hands out in front of him as he slowly inched toward the sound of Anna's voice. *Trip over a tie down and go over the side. That wouldn't be cool.*

"You keep talking too so I know where you are," Anna said.

One more step and Jake's hand touched Anna's upper arm and shoulder.

"I'm sorry I got ahead of you," Anna said. "I'm going to turn. Keep your hand on my shoulder and I'll walk you to the starboard hatch."

Jake still couldn't see a thing in the darkness. He put his trust on Anna and gripped her shoulder as she led him around the tower to the hatch.

Inside past the blackout and red-light area, Jake

could see once again. He lowered his hand off of Anna.

"Thanks for the help." *Thank you too, Lord.*

"No worries. I know my way around and I have excellent night vision. I should have been more attentive to you. Let's head up the ladder. I'll get you to the bridge and the XO."

Anna led the way up the ladder to the bridge. Looking forward through the glass Jake could barely see the outline of the flight deck.

"XO, Jake Huber reporting," PO2 Rodriguez said.

"Hi Jake," Commander John Looker, the XO of the USS Roosevelt, said peering over a map of the western Pacific Ocean.

"Good evening, Sir," Jake said.

"The Seahawk picked you up here," CDR Looker said pointing to the map. He then pointed to the area the Seahawk crew searched before their low fuel light demanded that they return to the ship. "An island didn't appear in this area either."

Jake didn't know why his island didn't show up on the map. He knew it existed out there, somewhere. He knew Sandy and David needed rescue from it. He knew he might be their one hope.

"As you can see, no islands show up in that area," the XO said. "That doesn't mean your island doesn't exist. Quite the contrary. We do come across islands that aren't on the map from time to time. We picked up a weak distress call from somewhere there. That caused a refocusing of rescue efforts to this area. We spotted you because of the refocusing."

"Thanks for believing me," Jake said.

"Chaplain Evans described you as reliable and trustworthy. He encouraged me to give you the benefit of the doubt and continue the search for the Taylors. Padre can be persuasive. The Australian authorities also confirmed the Taylors and their fishing boat have been missing for the past year. So, that lends credence to your story. Plus, both Chaplain Evans and Captain Hardy know your mom and want to help. So, I need you to give me as much intel as you can about your time in the water."

"Sandy and I went into the water off the north end of the island yesterday morning. We swam to the north for an hour and when I turned west Sandy turned back as we had agreed. After a while I realized a riptide combined with a storm and hours of treading water took me way west of the island. It's kind of ironic but my gut tells me where the Seahawk picked me up could very well be where I went into the water eleven days ago when I first found myself adrift. I don't remember how that happened to be. I'm hoping the crew of the Legacy can help me figure it out."

"I spoke with the skipper of the Legacy when we picked up the distress call. He told me you and another crew member went overboard in a storm. They picked up your crewmate but couldn't locate you. They called on everyone they could to join in the search. And yes, you're correct. The Seahawk picked you up in the same location that the Legacy said you and your crewmate went overboard."

Jake acknowledging the XO's smile said, "It's a God thing. Something I learned over the past eleven days. I can't explain it, but I believe it."

"Jake, you should know that there are many who don't believe your account of being on an island for nine days. When I verified that the Taylors were real and missing, I decided in your favor. Well, Padre's encouragement helped too. We can continue the search for another forty-eight hours. Whether we find the island or not, our mission requirements demand that we sail north at that time."

Disappointment reigned in Jake's mind and heart. The proof of the island's existence escaped them. His hope for a quick rescue of the Taylors faded even though his resolve to find them continued. He pictured Sandy in her cutoffs and tank top that first day on the island. She was strong and beautiful and he would never forget her. The vision of heaven 1.0 was etched in his mind to the depths of his soul. The papa bear hug of David Taylor before he left to swim around the island left its imprint.

• ● •

The Roosevelt sailed north as Jake waited for the Seahawk to take off. CDR Looker arranged for his transfer to the Legacy by helicopter. He would be lowered to the deck in a harness and tether like he had been rescued. Chaplain Evans shared with him the many times he went from ship to ship that way to provide Command Religious Program services to the crews that didn't have chaplains assigned. He called it the Holy Helo ride.

"We're ready for you on the Seahawk," Chief Jones said. "Too bad we couldn't find the island and rescue the Taylors."

Jake winced at the thought of not finding Sandy and David. A blast of exhaust from the helo returned his attention to the task at hand. He boarded the

Seahawk and strapped in under the watchful eyes of Chief Jones who closed the hatch and signaled the pilot for takeoff.

Jake knew the Legacy sailed near the Roosevelt. She and her crew also participated in the search for the Taylors since Jake's rescue. Jake spoke with the skipper of the Legacy by radio to set up the transfer. The skipper told him the rescue task would be left to the Australian Maritime Coast Guard and the Royal Australian Navy.

"Time to get you harnessed and ready," PO3 Corkeron said to Jake. "Seahawk will be over Legacy in two minutes. Legacy will heave-to so they can receive you by tether. It can be tricky to avoid the masts but Lt. Foley is the best and he plans to land you on the forward deck. Good luck and Godspeed."

"Thanks for all your help, Petty Officer. Please tell LT Foley he doesn't need to feel obligated to dunk me in the water before he puts me on the deck of the Legacy. Padre told me that happens sometimes as a rite of passage for chaplains. Just tell him I'm not a chaplain."

Hovering above Legacy's forward deck, Jake heard Chief Jones give the order, "Connect the tether and prepare to lower away."

Jake stepped into the doorway, leaning against the pull of the tether. Through his headset he heard Chief Jones say, "Lower away," and his descent began.

"He's on target right over the bow," the Chief said to LT Foley. "Ten feet, five feet, he's on the deck, hold her steady."

"Roger that," the Lt. replied.

Two Legacy crewmembers grounded Jake to

prevent static shock, disconnected the harness and signaled a thumbs-up to the Seahawk. The hoist recalled the tether and harness and the Seahawk flew off, returning to the Roosevelt.

———•●•———

"Welcome aboard, Jake," First Mate Ian McDaniels said. Jake looked at the barrel-chested Aussie with decades of sea time. Mac put the crew trainees through their paces every day.

"Hey Mac," Jake said. "I'm glad to be back. Did I pass the man-overboard drill?"

"I have to say that we all thought you were a goner. You hold the new record for the Legacy surviving two weeks overboard. We found your cohort in crime the same night the two of you went over the side. Stubby's fine, by the way."

"Chaplain Evans shared that with me on the Roosevelt. But I still have no idea what happened that night. The first thing I remember is treading water at sunrise and not knowing how I got there or where there was. From what I can piece together my memory begins the morning after I went into the water. So, I'm missing that whole night."

"Talk to Stubby and he'll fill you in. We've been one man short in the crew watch rotation while you've been away. Every member volunteered to pick up one extra watch. They'll all be glad you're back. Your first watch starts after noon chow. That'll give you time to talk with Stubby and refresh your memory. The Captain wants you to touch base with him, too."

"Aye Aye. I'll go see the Captain right away. Then

I'll change out of these Navy dungarees and into proper crewing clothes. I'll meet up with Stubby for chow and get my memory up to speed. Before I go, tell me if you got the word about my time on the island."

"The Captain told us about it and even involved us in the search for it. Haven't found it so far."

"I survived for ten days on an island that no one can find. It's out there with two people on it in need of rescue. Do we have any time to continue the search?"

"Ask the Captain when you see him. He decides where we sail and when. Now, be on your way."

"Aye Aye."

Jake went down below deck towards the captain's quarters, passing the small galley. Stubby sat at a table eating the standard lunch fare of sandwich and fruit. He served as a fellow trainee like Jake.

"Hey, Jake," Stubby said, looking up. "Where you been hanging lately?"

"Hey," Jake said. "I spent some time on an island and an aircraft carrier. Mac said we went overboard during a storm. Problem is, I don't remember it. I can't remember how I ended up in the water. What happened?"

"Sure. Get some food and I'll talk while you eat."

Jake decided to eat first and see the captain after. He made a ham, turkey, salami, lettuce, tomato and mustard sandwich on seven grain bread, grabbed an apple and chocolate milk and sat down with Stubby.

"So, fill me in.

"Do you remember being down below in our bunks playing video games?"

"I sort of remember that much. My next memory is treading water in the open sea. It's the part in between I can't come up with."

"The all-hands-on-deck call came down. We hit the ladder to go up on deck. You climbed up first, followed by me. Just as we came through the hatch and before we even had a chance to hook up our safety straps, a huge wave broke over the deck. I grabbed you but the force of it took us both over the side. We got separated when we hit the water. I thought maybe you drowned. The waves tossed me around like a rag doll and even though the crew heaved to and went into 'man overboard' it took a while to get to me. We searched all night for you. At one point early on, Mac tossed a survival bag over the side. He said with a little luck you and it would meet up. We searched for you for days. The captain couldn't call for assistance because the wave that took us over the side shorted out the radio. It took a while for a response to the distress beacon. When a Royal Australian Navy ship came along side, they supplied the parts to get the radio fixed and a full-scale search got underway. A few days ago, one of the search ships picked up a faint mayday call. That redirected the search. Two days ago, a message came that you had been rescued and taken aboard the Roosevelt. I couldn't believe it. And now seeing you, I have to say you don't look like you spent ten days treading water in the ocean."

"The truth is, I didn't," Jake said. "I spent most of the time on an island with two shipwreck survivors, a truly beautiful girl and her fisherman father. A tsunami sank their fishing boat a year ago. That survival bag that Mac tossed over the side also made it to the island. I signaled on the radio several times. I guess my signal finally redirected the search. How I came to be rescued is a whole other story. I still hope we can find the island and rescue the Taylors."

"Wow! What a story. We can talk more later, it's time to get back on deck. When are you back into the rotation?"

"Right after I report to the Captain. You guys have been shorthanded long enough. Let's get to it."

Chapter Sixteen

"**Dad, it's been** two days since Jake left." Sandy said. "I know he's ok because God has a plan for him beyond this island. But I can't help thinking he might need help. My strength is back and I feel fine, so I thought I'd swim to the south end of the island and see what I can find. What do you think?"

"I think you're going to do what you are going to do," David said. "I'll pray for your safety and your safe return. You will be coming back, right?"

"Of course I will," Sandy laughingly said. "Hopefully with Jake as soon as I can. I'll go in the morning."

"Well then let's have a good dinner and a good night's rest and get you off first thing in the morning."

"I have it on good authority that there will be coconut crusted fried fish, clams and fruit for dinner," Sandy said. "It's the chef's specialty."

"I can't wait," David said.

A beautiful sunrise greeted Sandy at daybreak. The warm tropical breeze made the calm cool water feel good as she swam. Dolphins swam alongside her enticing her to grab hold of their dorsal fin so they could propel her along.

Lord, the dolphins are a good taxi service like Jake said. At this rate I'll be around the island in no time. Thanks for the lift.

In no time at all, Sandy walked out of the cool blue water into the heat of the day. She arrived at the beach where she had first found Jake. *Where could he be?*

She walked through her camp. *Everything's in order.*

She headed up to the cave room. Jake told her he'd stowed the survival bag and other gear there. She found the bag and gear, but no Jake.

Lord, where is he? Maybe by the pond.

The lush fruitful trees enticed her. She grabbed a papaya and ate it as she walked. Arriving at the pond, she went to the falls and rinsed the sea from herself and took a long drink of the fresh water. Still no sign of Jake and that worried her. She decided to rest by the pond and eat a little more fruit before she grabbed the gear and swam back to the north end of the island.

In her heart Sandy knew Jake never arrived on this southern end of the island or the gear would be gone.

"Lord, I don't know what's happened to Jake, but You do," Sandy prayed. "Please keep him safe wherever he is. I leave him in Your hands knowing how much You love him. Help me swim back around to the north end with the gear. The dolphin taxi service would be helpful too. Thanks for all You do. I love you, Lord."

Well rested, Sandy went to the cave room. She checked to make sure the items were in their waterproof bags. Fastening her pot to the outside of the bag she picked it up and headed for the water.

Sandy and the survival bag made their way around

to the north end of the island early in the afternoon. The dolphins again assisted with taxi service and kept her safe from sharks.

———•●•———

David spent the day watching for Sandy from the shore. He spotted the yellow bag first and then Sandy. "Thank You, Lord for bringing her back safe. I don't see Jake with her. Wherever he is, please keep him safe."

Chapter Seventeen

Aboard the Legacy, Jake served as look-out while the boat sailed through the assigned search grid near the USS Roosevelt. Sailors aboard both vessels watched for the island Jake had been on with the Taylors. The calm sea and the bright sun matched the warm day making conditions for searching the best.

"Lord, help us find the island," Jake prayed as he scanned the horizon. "You and I both know it exists. You've kept the Taylors safe and provided for their needs. You put me on that island to open my eyes to You and help with their rescue too. I believe you will help them. Use me to do that."

After a long and unsuccessful final search day, Jake heard Mac set the night watch. The Captain set a course to have the Legacy arrive back at Kaneohe, K-bay, by the training course end date. Jake and his crewmates would be home in time to start the new school year.

"I thought we would find the island," Jake said to Stubby as he laid in his bunk.

"Are you sure you stayed on an island and didn't dream it all up?" Stubby asked.

"I know the difference between the island and the

visions or dreams that I had while on it. Look, you're not a religious guy. I get it. But I gotta tell you, what I saw and experienced changed my life forever."

"What are you talking about?"

"When I first landed on the island, I found myself up in the air and saw my unconscious self lying on the beach. Three angels floated there with me, talking with me about Jesus and heaven. They told me God wanted them to keep me safe and help me find my purpose."

"Ok?"

"I hear the skepticism in your voice. But the truth is I saw the Lord in heaven for real."

"You mean in a dream, right?"

"More like a vision than a dream. The difference is that one's real and one's not. I saw all the people who died believing in Jesus as the Savior of the world standing before the throne of God. Jesus was there on that throne. That's where they are until Jesus comes back here when the resurrection happens. That's when the earth is changed and all His followers will live on the new earth with Jesus forever. The good news is that He wants everyone to be there. The bad news is that some will choose not to be there by not believing in Him."

"I don't think you should say any of that to the rest of the guys till we're back at K-bay," Stubby cautioned. "I mean I hear you and we can talk about all this, but they might decide to throw you overboard again just to see if this God can save you. Personally, I think you hit your head going over the side and had a ten daydream while floating in the ocean. The only question in my mind is how you're in such good physical shape after ten days in the water. You should have been shark bait at best."

"Back before we went overboard, I would've agreed with you," Jake said. "If you told me what I told you I would've said you're full of it. But you know me and I'm telling you that I experienced and observed reality from Sandy Taylor and her dad to Mic, Ace and Cal the three angels. I bet my life on it and here I am. I have a lot more to tell you but we've got early watch in the morning, so we'd better get some shut eye."

"You're my friend, Jake. The whole crew respects the fact that you survived ten days overboard. Just cut us some slack. Give us time to process your story."

———— • ● • ————

Coarse language was a given on a Bargues class A training vessel with a crew of fifteen veterans and fifteen trainees. It never bothered Jake before. He could match any man in the foul mouth department. The Marines Jake hung out with used a lot of foul language but had enough self-discipline that they could shut it off around women and children, a skill Jake exercised as well.

Now the foul mouth talk bothered Jake. Something inside reacted negatively when he heard it from others around him.

Lord, I know I feel this way because I'm Yours. Should I say something to my crewmates? I wonder what Sandy would do. I bet she would be honest and real.

Jake and Stubby relieved of their watch duties met in the galley for coffee. They sat across the table from one of the veteran crewmates, Pete. He knew more about sailing, rope and knots than anyone Jake had ever met. He droned on using colorfully coarse language about one of the other trainees who left a trailing rope a mess.

"No offense, Pete," Jake said. "Since my overboard experience that kind of language really bothers me. I'd really appreciate it if you would tone it down a little."

"What are you talking about?" Pete asked. "We all talk that way. Even you."

"I know. I'm just trying to clean my act up and would appreciate it if you would do me this favor."

"He experienced some kind of spiritual awakening," Stubby said trying to help his friend.

"No worries," Pete said. "I'll try to clean it up around you but no promises."

"Thanks, Pete. It means a lot to me."

Mac, standing outside the galley overheard the conversation. He came in, got a cup of coffee and sat down next to Jake.

"You know," Mac said to Jake. "It's been my experience that most blokes don't realize the language they use day to day. When made aware of it, they can choose better. They can also choose not to. Either way it comes down to their level of respect for the bloke they're talking to. That's why they can clean up how they talk around women and children."

"That's very inciteful of you," Pete said. "Just like tying knots. A bloke can tie them tight and clean or loose and sloppy like that dingo, Kent. I showed him the difference. Now it's his choice. And I'll box his ears if he makes the wrong choice again."

"Easy, Mate," Mac said. "Remember, we run a

training cruise."

"I know," Pete said with a smile. "Just kidding, sorta."

———•●•———

The southern trade winds kept the Legacy running along at an average speed of 14+ knots. Following seas, having the wind at your back, made for much better sailing than into the northern trade winds. It would take the Legacy twice as long to get to Kaneohe fighting headwinds and a current on a more northern route. Jake overheard the Captain tell Mac they would sail to French Polynesia and then head north to the Hawaiian Islands. The Legacy would be at K-Bay well before high school classes started. That made Jake happy even though every day they sailed farther away from Sandy and her dad.

"Jake," Mac yelled. "The Captain wants a word. He's at the helm presently."

"Aye, aye," Jake said, finishing the tightening of the main sheet lines.

"Do you know what he wants?" Jake asked Mac as he passed by him.

"He didn't say."

Captain Clark, a no-nonsense sailor, desired to pass on the love and know-how of sailing to the next generation. Jake read the care and concern in his eyes when he met with him after he came back aboard the Legacy following his rescue.

As Jake approached the helm, Captain Clark instructed the Helmsman trainee on the course to follow.

"Captain, you wanted to see me," Jake said.

"Yes Jake," the Captain said, nudging Jake by the elbow a few steps aft of the wheel. "I received a radio message this morning from the XO of MCB Hawaii. He's an old friend of mine. He told me about a security threat to the base from someone working within the high school crowd. He wants to know if you would be willing to work undercover for base security to help them ferret it out. Basically, they want you to keep your eyes and ears open for anything or anyone out of the ordinary. They know reporters will be all over you regarding your overboard experience and rescue. They think you might be able to pick up on someone due to the high-profile exposure. The men from your dad's old unit suggested you were perfect for this. If you're willing to help, security will set it all up with you prior to our arrival at K-Bay. What do you think?"

"Wow. They really think I can help?"

"Jake, you've had more training than most young Marines. Not to mention you just survived 10 days overboard regardless of the circumstances, on an island or not. I agree with your young Marine friends. You're the guy."

"If base security thinks I can be helpful to them, I'm more than happy to try. Just one thing, Captain. I'm not giving up on finding the island that the Taylors are stranded on. I'd like to talk with you more about that some time before we dock at K-Bay."

"I welcome the conversation, Jake. In the meantime, keep our talk to yourself. I'll radio the XO of your willingness to help and let you know when I hear back from him or base security."

Jake left the captain and headed down to the galley

for chow. He found Stubby there dishing a plate full of spaghetti and meatballs. The garlic bread smelled great. And the apple crisp for dessert reminded him of island mango and papaya deserts.

"I have to say," Stubby said, "We certainly don't go hungry on this boat."

"Don't tell me," Jake said. "Tell the cook. I'm sure a complement like that would go a long way with him."

Jake dished his spaghetti and meatballs, grabbed a piece of garlic bread and sat down next to Stubby.

"Sounds like we'll be back at K-Bay in time for the start of football practice," Jake said.

Stubby nodded his head with a mouth full of spaghetti. He and Jake had become close friends over the past two years. Both Marine brats enjoyed playing sports together and had each other's backs through the first two years of high school.

"I'll be glad to get my feet on dry land again," Stubby said. "Don't get me wrong, crewing this boat has been a blast except for the overboard part. Thanks for dragging me along with you."

"What? I didn't drag you," Jake said. "As I remember you begged me to see if I could get you on the crew."

"Yea, I know," Stubby said biting off a piece of bread. "Just pulling your line."

"One thing for sure," Jake said. "I learned a lot on this boat, and on the island I survived on."

"You're not gonna let that go, are you?"

"No, I'm not. The Taylors are still stranded there and I'm the only one who knows it. I've gotta figure out a way to get them rescued. Sandy was instrumental in helping me get acquainted with God. I owe her for that, and more."

"Well bro, if I can do anything, let me know."

Jake heard Stubby's words but in his mind he sat on an island watching a beautiful girl sitting on the beach in the moonlight beneath a sky full of stars.

Coming back to reality Jake said, "God has a plan for me, Stubby. I don't know the details, yet. But I trust Him with my life."

"When you figure it out, let me know. In the meantime, I need you to tell me more about this God thing of yours. But after I get a couple of hours in the rack."

"Yea, I'm with you," Jake said. "Let's get some shuteye."

The Legacy sailed north from French Polynesia in the home stretch of her cruise to K-Bay. Mac told Jake Captain Clark wanted to see him in his quarters after evening chow. The boat sailed one day away from anchor at K-Bay.

Jake knocked on the captain's door.

"Hey skipper, Mac said you wanted to see me."

"Come in Jake. Have a seat. I received some news from the Marine security unit at MCBH at Kaneohe. Apparently, they've become aware of an Asian agent posing as a high school student near the base. The security folks don't know what she's up to. They're concerned because as a student near the base she has access to base personnel and the base itself, particularly the air wing. They want you to keep an eye out for her or anything out of the ordinary. If you see or hear of anything, you're supposed to contact SSgt. James from base security at this number."

The Captain gave a slip of paper with the number

on it to Jake.

"Put that number into you cell phone when you get back to your rack, and deep six the paper."

"Aye aye, sir."

Jake knew SSgt. Leroy James and considered him a close friend. They spent a lot of time together when Jake's dad died in the accident. A big guy, he grew up in a Louisiana bayou and could survive in any hot spot you put him in. *I can work with him any day.*

"Anything else, Captain?" Jake asked.

"That's all for now. When you get ashore tomorrow be aware. The media will be all over you and your mom whenever you're off base. Now, get some rest until your watch starts."

"Aye aye, sir."

Jake made his way to his berth. There he found Stubby lying on his bunk playing a video game. Their two bunk mates already went up on deck for their duty.

"What you been up to?" Stubby asked.

"I had a meeting with the captain."

"What did he want with you?"

"He gave me a message from base security at K-Bay. He told me to keep it to myself, but I might as well share it with you. You're with me all the time anyway. Seems they heard about an Asian agent working the base posing as a high school student. They want me to keep my eyes and ears open and see if I can spot her. The way I figure it, four eyes see twice as much as two. You in?"

"I am absolutely in. No matter what I've got your six."

Chapter Eighteen

"**What is that** big smile all over your face?" Stubby asked Jake as the Legacy dropped anchor in K-Bay just beyond He'eia Kea Boat Harbor.

"Tropical sunshine, calm water and humid air make it a great day to be in port," Jake said.

Lord, you are the most important thing I learned about this summer. I'm not sure yet what that all means for the future, but I'm sure you'll help me figure it out. I wish I could talk with Sandy. She would be a big help with that.

"Hey, Jake," Stubby yelled. "The supply barge is coming along side. Mac wants us to help secure it and unload it. Then we can ride it back to the harbor."

"Let's getter done," Jake said.

The barge full of supplies for the next Legacy sail pulled up. It had fruits and vegetables, gallons of water, cans of coffee and everything else the cook ordered. There would be a new crew of trainees. They would be waiting at the harbor for the barge to bring them to the Legacy.

"You are no longer trainees," Captain Clark said. "From now on we consider you full-fledged sailors. You'll be welcome to sail on any boat. You all did a great job and I salute you. Mac take'em home."

"Grab your duffel bags and get on the barge," Mac said.

Fifteen newly trained crew members including Jake and Stubby followed suit and loaded onto the barge with their gear.

"It's been great working with you," Jake said, passing by Mac. "I learned a lot from you."

"I've only known ya fer a few months, but I can tell you're special," Mac said. "Not just because you survived your overboard experience either. If I can ever be of help to ya, lemme know."

"There is one thing you could do for me. When you're sailing around where I went overboard keep a sharp eye out for that uncharted island. Two people on it need rescue."

"I'll watch out," Mac said.

———•●•———

Jake, along with Stubby and his crewmates, threw his bags off the barge and onto the dock. There stood fifteen incoming trainees for the next cruise standing by to load their gear and board the barge for the Legacy. The new group of trainees consisted of girls with several older women. *I'll have to ask Mac about that cruise sometime.* He and Stubby grabbed their bags and headed up the dock with the other new sailors toward a sea of family members and those waiting for them. Mac told them the Captain radioed ahead the Legacy's estimated time of arrival so transportation would be arranged.

As they approached the shoreline Jake heard a

familiar voice holler, "Hey swabbie, need a ride?"

SSgt. Leroy James, his friend from MCBH base security office, greeted him. He wore civilian clothes, an odd sight for a duty day.

"Hey Jarhead," Jake said smiling. "Good to see you too."

"I told your mom I'd pick you up, so she wouldn't have to take off work. Besides, I had an ulterior motive to see you. That thing your captain talked to you about."

"Leroy, this is Stubby my best friend," Jake said. "I told him about the thing since we pretty much do everything together anyway."

"Hi Stubby, good to meet you."

"Good to meet you too," Stubby said. "I've got Jake's back, so it'll be good to know what's going on."

"I can't overemphasize the need for keeping this just between us," Leroy said. "Let's stow your gear in my truck and head for the base. I want to bring you up to speed on the latest intel. We'll take the back way out of here due to all the paparazzi waiting for you out front. I need to share some info with you before you become a public news story. We'll talk in the truck."

Once free of the harbor, Leroy pulled over to the shoulder.

"Our intel folks updated us this morning," Leroy said. "They recently discovered that the agent we're looking for is an Asian female posing as a high school junior at Kalaheo High School. They think that her mission is to disrupt base IT and communications for what purpose they're not sure yet."

"What exactly do you want us to do?" Jake asked.

"We're counting on you to help us identify the

agent. We'll take it from there. She will be a new student this year. I'll get a list to you of those coming in Permanent Change of Station (PCS). That'll help narrow down the possibilities."

"We get new students all the time," Stubby said. "Whoever she is, she'll either be outgoing joining clubs and organizations, or be a quiet mousey nerd type and keep out of the spotlight. In either case do we have any type of time constraint we're working against?"

"As of now, we need to identify her ASAP," Leroy said, "since the end game is unknown. Once the press gets hold of you, Jake, most likely at the main gate, they'll provide helpful publicity and that'll draw students to you. That's a tool you can use to your advantage."

"What do you mean?" Jake asked.

"Your publicity will put you in front of people, particularly your classmates. You can use it to engage them in conversation and stuff like that."

"Ok. I can do that," Jake said.

"I wrote down a phone number you can use to contact me directly, anytime," Leroy said, handing Jake a business card. He gave one to Stubby too.

As they approached the main gate to MCBH a television crew with a camera truck made note of everyone entering. The gate guard waved Leroy through the gate and on to the base because of his base sticker on the windshield.

"Glad we didn't have to deal with reporters yet," Stubby said. "I just wanna get home, get a shower and a pile of tacos from the food truck."

"Yeah. I need to see mom and show her I'm okay," Jake said. "A shower and food are on my list too. I want to see Chaplain Evans too."

"You'll need to meet with the press soon and get that ball rolling," Leroy said. "Remember the task at hand. Football starts next week, right?"

"Yeah man. Double sessions and weight training," Stubby said with a sarcastic grin. "Can't wait."

Leroy pulled the truck up into Jake's driveway. Karen Huber ran out of the house followed by Chaplain Evans.

"You're home! You're home!" Karen said, pulling the truck door open.

Jake stepped out of the truck into the waiting arms of his mom. They exchanged a hug and a kiss and another hug.

"I'm so happy you're home and safe," Karen said. "Padre came over to wait for you with me. He told me more about your overboard experience but I want to hear all about from you, about the island and the Taylors and the angels and Jesus."

"I'll tell you everything Mom," Jake said. "First, let's send Stubby and Leroy on their way."

"Oh, Stubby, how are you?" Karen asked, giving him a big hug. "I'm glad you're home and safe too. Leroy, thanks for picking up the boys," Karen said.

"No problem, Karen. Glad to do it"

Jake grabbed his gear from the truck bed. Leroy and Stubby drove away down the street toward Stubby's.

"Sounds like the rest of your sail went according to training plan," Padre said. "I think you learned a lot more than you figured on."

"Definitely didn't get bored," Jake said. "Plus, my vision of Jesus in heaven changed my life. I'm worried about Sandy and David Taylor and trying to figure out a way to get them rescued. I ask Jesus to help them every day, but I feel I should do more.”

“Prayer is the most important thing you can do,” Padre said. “We have no idea about God’s plan in the grand scheme of things. But I’m certain He’s got their best interest at heart.”

“Jake, come inside and tell me all about your summer under sail,” Karen said. “Padre, please join us. I know Jake told you his story on the Roosevelt but we would love to have you stay for dinner.”

“I’d love to Karen,” Padre said. “And Jake, I’d like to hear your account of heaven again. I’ve had some time to reflect on what you told me on the Roosevelt. I have a few questions I’d like to ask about your visions.”

Jake picked up his gear and led the way into the house. Padre held the door open for Karen and followed her in.

“I’ve got fried chicken warming in the oven, homemade potato salad and watermelon wedges in the fridge,” Karen said. “How about we eat while we talk?”

“Great plan, Mom,” Jake said. “I’ll never pass up your fried chicken and potato salad.”

“Sounds good to me too,” Padre said.

Karen placed the fried chicken on the table next to the potato salad and watermelon and sat down across from Jake at the four-sided kitchen table. Padre sat on another side between them.

“Mom, this smells so good, “Jake said. “I can’t wait to dig in.”

“How about if I offer a prayer of thanks to the Lord before we get started?” Padre asked.

“Sure thing Padre,” Jake said. “And also for a safe

return home."

"You read my mind," Padre said.

After the prayer, all three filled their plates and enjoyed Jake's first home-cooked meal since he'd left for his sailing adventure, except for the island cuisine. As the three ate, Jake shared with his mom about his overboard experience, complete with angels, visions of heaven and Jesus, and the Taylors.

"David and Sandy, two really great people, follow the teachings of Jesus. They follow Jesus in a way I've never experienced," Jake said. "The hardest thing is trying to figure out how to get them rescued. We can't locate the island they got stranded on."

"Jake, what an amazing story," Karen said.

"Not a story, Mom. It happened. It's real. The angel Mic even told me dad stood there, one of the many before the throne of Jesus."

"Your vision intrigues me Jake," Padre said. "Can you remember any more details about it?"

"Sorry, Padre. I couldn't look but for a glance because of the brightness of the whole scene."

"Well, if you ever remember anything else, please share it with me."

"Sure thing, Padre," Jake said. "Can you do something for me? As you talk with Captain Hardy or others sailing in the area where I went overboard, would you ask them to look for the island and the Taylors?"

"Can do," Padre said.

Chapter Nineteen

Jake walked up to Stubby's car and dropped his bag. He stretched his arms and back muscles. *Double session first day is always grueling no matter how much a player prepares.*

"I'm glad that one's in the book," Stubby said, unlocking the doors to his car. "How about we head to the beach for a cool down. We might run into some of the girls, too."

"My mom doesn't get home from work for a couple of hours, so dinner will be later," Jake said. "Let's get something to eat on the way."

"You read my mind bro," Stubby said. "It'll also be your first opportunity for interaction with people besides our football buds."

"What do you mean by that?" Jake asked.

"You know, the secret agent girl we're supposed to be watching for."

"Oh, that."

"Yeah, that."

"Let's go to the drive-thru for chocolate shakes and fries," Jake said. "Then on to the beach."

"Will do," Stubby said.

"Not too busy," Jake said as they pulled up to the

window.

"Hey Sheila," Stubby said. "Two chocolate shakes and two large fries. Jake and I need an energy boost before we head to the beach."

"Coming right up," Sheila said. "Jan and Carson drove through a while ago heading there too. So, you might see them."

"Hey Sheila," Jake said. "Long time no see."

"Hi Jake. I hear your summer crewing training turned into quite the adventure."

"Yeah. I'll tell you about it when we have a little more time."

"Here you go," Sheila said. "Your order's up. Enjoy, and enjoy the beach too."

"Oh, we will," Stubby said, pulling away.

The road to the Marine Corps Base Hawaii beach had little traffic on a weekday afternoon. The parking lot by the beach looked empty but for a couple of cars.

"That looks like Jan's old Mustang convertible," Stubby said. "She drives one hot looking car."

Stubby parked by Jan's car. Jake and Stubby walked off the parking lot onto a sand path.

"I like how the grassy sand rolls down to the beach and then opens up to the ocean," Jake said as the two of them walked through it to the beach.

Stubby spotted Jan and Carson. "Hey!"

The girls waved at them.

"What a gorgeous day," Stubby said as he and Jake walked over to them.

"The water must feel great today," Jake said, noting Carson's wet hair still dripping.

"Great for a Monday afternoon in August," Carson said.

Seeing Carson with her long blond hair reminded Jake of Sandy and his time on the island with her.

Stubby grabbed Jake's arm and pulled him along. "Let's hit the waves."

Coming back to the present, Jake raced Stubby to the water and dove in. They swam out beyond the breakwater where they floated around for a while.

"You know what?" Jake asked. "This swim hits the spot after our first day of double sessions. Cool water and a breeze help me relax in a great way."

"Right on, bro. By the way, what held you so deep in thought that I had to almost drag you into the water?"

"Believe it or not, Carson's long blond dripping wet hair reminded me of Sandy and took me back to the island."

"Carson is a pretty girl," Stubby said. "She's smart too."

"True enough," Jake said, all the while remembering his beautiful Sandy.

Just then a pod of dolphins swam by. They swam close enough that the boys could've touched them.

That one looks just like the one I swam with while I was stranded on the island with Sandy. No. It couldn't be. Could it? It would be a stretch that Ace directed the dolphins to follow along from the island. Could they be around just in case?

"Why don't you ask Carson to the dance on Friday?" Stubby said interrupting Jake's thought. "You ask her and I'll ask Jan and we can double up."

"I like that idea. It'll be our first real opportunity to mix and mingle off base. Maybe we can get a line on secret agent girl. Let's head in."

Jake got to the shore ahead of Stubby, passing Jan

who was on her way out into the water. He sat down next to Carson.

"You two enjoy yourselves out there?"

"We sure did," Jake said. "A great way to cool down after practice. And, we came up with a good idea. Do you want to go to the Friday night dance with me? We can double up with Stubby and Jan if she agrees to go with him."

"I'd love to go with you. It'll be fun. Jan will say yes to Stubby. We should let her drive. Her dad'll be more comfortable with that. She could put the top down for an added bonus."

"Ok. I'll pick up Stubby and swing by your house and get you. Then we can head over to Jan's."

"There is one thing," Carson said. "You'll have to come in and say hi to my parents. They gotta do their parent thing and check you out."

"No worries. I like your parents. They're cool."

"Taking out daddy's only daughter makes him a little intimidating," Carson said.

"How many guys have you gone out with?"

"You'll be the second one. Justin took me out to watch the surfing competition last month. Dad made it rough on him. But he didn't know my dad either."

"Your dad acts a lot like mine did," Jake said. He remembered how his dad and MSgt. Koke, Carson's dad, served in the same unit for many years. "He wants you to be safe. I'm sure it'll be fine."

Stubby and Jan came up and sat down with the two of them.

"Jan said she would go to the dance with me," Stubby said with a big smile. "How about you two? Go with us and make it a double?"

"For sure," Carson said. "We also thought that Jan should drive, with the top down of course. What do you think, Jan?"

"I like it," Jan said. "My dad will like it too. He trusts my driving more than anyone else my age. No offense guys."

"None taken." Stubby said. "I like the idea of going to a dance in the summer with the top down on the car."

Jake bumped Carson with his shoulder and said, "I'll text you details later in the week."

"Ok. Sounds good." Carson said.

"Stubby, let's you and I hit the road," Jake said. "My mom will be getting dinner and we don't want to be late."

"Ok. What are we having?"

"It's one of your favorites. Hamburgers and pork & beans with mac & cheese."

"Let's git," Stubby said.

Chapter Twenty

"This has been one ball-busting week," Stubby said to Jake as they drove to pick up Carson at her house. "When we get to Carson's, you can go in and do the 'meet the girl's dad' bit. I'll wait in the car."

"I planned on that," Jake said. "Besides, when we get to Jan's you get to meet with her dad while Carson and I wait outside by her car."

"No, I think you two should come in with me. Then her dad might go easier on me."

"Gunny Sgt. McBride will give you the full dad treatment. Nothing slides when it comes to his daughter. So, Carson and I will just wait outside."

"You're no help."

"You've got this Stubby."

Pulling into Carson's driveway Jake said, "Wish me luck."

"No worries. Carson's dad loves you."

"Yeah, but I've never taken his daughter out on a date before. I've got a feeling that might change things a bit."

"Yeah, but a double date might make him go easier on you."

"I don't know," Jake said. "You and I together

might make it worse."

"Ha!"

Jake got out of the car and went to the door and knocked. Carson's mom came to the door and invited him in.

"Hi, Jake, come on in," Mrs. Koke said.

"Hey, Mrs. Koke. I'm here to pick up Carson."

"She's not quite ready. Have a seat. I'm sure she'll be right down."

Jake sat in a padded chair next to the sofa. A neatly kept room decorated in a Hawaiian motif surrounded him.

"Hi, Jake," MSgt. Koke said. "So, you want to take my daughter to the dance tonight."

"Yes sir," Jake said.

"You're a responsible young man. So, I expect you to treat Carson with respect and have her home by midnight and not a second later. I'll be waiting for her to come in and I need my sleep because I have an o dark thirty appointment that you don't want me to be tired for. Am I clear?"

"Yes, sir.

"Good. I'm glad we understand each other. By the way, make sure the four of you have a good time tonight."

"Yes sir. Thank you, sir."

After a long silent pause, a smiling MSgt. Koke said, "Relax Jake. As a dad I had to say all those things. I know you well enough that I'm not worried at all. Please don't prove me wrong."

Before Jake could answer, Carson came into the room. Wearing a yellow floral sundress, she looked stunning. Once again, his mind took him back to thoughts of Sandy. *I wonder why Carson reminds me so much of Sandy.*

"*Remember.*" Jake heard the whisper in his mind. The word startled him and took him back to the island and the vision through the shimmering crease.

"Hey, where did you go?" Carson asked noting the look on Jake's face.

"Oh, hey," Jake said. "You really look nice."

"Okay, you two," MSgt. Koke said. "I think you've kept Stubby waiting in the car long enough."

The two needed no more urging. They snapped a few photos and headed out the door.

"I began to wonder if I was ever going to see you two again." Stubby said. "We need to rock and roll."

Carson and Jake got in the back seat and let Stubby be their chauffeur to Jan's house. His ride compared to riding in an Uber. Jan's convertible would be cooler.

Stubby pulled up in front of the house and the three got out. Jake and Carson walked over to Jan's Mustang and leaned against it. Stubby headed toward the front door.

"Suck it up," Jake yelled. Carson elbowed him in the side for the big smile on his face.

———•●•———

Stubby knocked on the front door and Mrs. McBride let him in.

"Jan'll be down in a minute," she said. "Why don't you have a seat in the living room."

A bright and airy room greeted him. It had a Hawaiian motif like many he had seen before. Before he could sit down on the sofa, Gunny Sgt. McBride came into the room.

"So, you want to take my daughter to the dance," GSgt. McBride said.

"Yes, I do," Stubby said with a crackly voice. *Calm down man. You're way too nervous.*

"I have some basic rules you'll have to follow," Gunny said. "First and foremost, you will treat my daughter with respect."

"Yes, I will," Stubby said. *If he's trying to intimidate me, he has totally succeeded.*

"You will have her home by midnight and not a second later," Gunny said. "I know she's driving but I'm holding you responsible.

"Home by midnight, yes sir," Stubby said feeling about four feet tall.

"Finally, I want you to have a good time," Gunny said with a big smile on his face. Stubby wasn't sure how to take that.

"Lighten up," Gunny said. "I know you came with Jake and Carson so I'm sure everything will be on the up and up. Besides, I work for your dad and I know him well enough to know if you're anything like him, you are a class act."

"Thank you, sir," Stubby said.

"Here she comes," Mrs. McBride said, as Jan came down the stairway and into the living room.

"Wow!" Stubby said. She wore a pink outfit that contrasted with her tan and her dark brown hair. "You look amazing."

"Thanks," Jan said. "Let's take some pics and get on our way. I'm sure Jake and Carson want to get going."

"Let's git," Stubby said.

Stubby opened the driver's side door for Jan, letting Jake slip into the back seat. He ran around and did the same for Carson. Jan drove with Stubby, riding shotgun. He could tell that Jake and Carson enjoyed being chauffeured again. Four friends off to a school dance.

Chapter Twenty-one

"The parking lot looks as full as a school day," Jan said, pulling into a parking spot.

"I wonder how many new kids we have this year," Stubby said.

"And how many are Marine Corps brats like us and how many are from town?" Jake asked, thinking about the Asian girl spy he needed to identify.

"Let's go in and find out," Carson said.

"Come on," Jan said. "We're fashionably late and it sounds like the music has started."

The four made their way to the gym that had been nicely decorated with palm trees and Hawaiian flowers. The front row of the bleachers on both sides provided seating. A DJ stood in the corner playing tunes over the speaker system and had the place hopping.

Carson pulled Jake by the arm into the mass of kids moving to the beat. Stubby and Jan followed along and they danced.

After a while, the DJ stopped the music. "I'm going to take a ten-minute break," he said. "They tell me your favorite snacks and sodas can be found on the tables in the back, so enjoy."

Jake and Carson made their way to the food and

drink tables. Jimmy Smith, a sophomore member of the student newspaper, stopped Jake.

"I heard about your ten-day ocean survival ordeal," Jimmy said. "I want to do an article on you for the paper. Will you tell me your story?"

This will be a great opportunity. If I play my cards right, I can use it to identify the newbies.

"You talk to Jimmy," Carson said. "I'll grab us some sodas." And off she went.

A group of kids gathered around Jake and Jimmy as Jake shared the events of the past summer. Holding back on the angels and visions, Jake ended saying, "One thing I'm certain of. God is real. If not for Him I wouldn't be here. I'll save that story for another time."

"Ok," Jimmy said. "I'll hold you to it."

———— • ● • ————

As Jake told his story, Stubby stayed back with Jan watching the kids. He spotted a girl he'd never seen before. She stood back from the group but appeared extremely interested in Jake. *I wonder if she's the spy?*

Stubby nudged Jan and they walked over to the new girl.

"Hi, I'm Stubby and this is Jan. We wanted to introduce ourselves."

"Hi. I'm Mae Ling. Everyone calls me Mae. My mom and I moved here over the summer. She works in real estate and started a new office here."

"We're both juniors," Jan said.

"Oh, so am I," Mae said. "It's kind of a bummer starting at a new high school my junior year. My mom says I have to deal with it."

"Do you know that boy over there?" Mae asked.

"That would be Jake," Stubby said. "He and I crewed on a sailing boat this past summer. We went overboard during a storm. They found me right away. It took ten days before they pulled Jake from the water and a couple more till he got back aboard our boat."

"Ten days in the water and he survived," Mae said. "Quite impressive."

"Well, he says part of the time he spent on an island with two other people," Stubby said. "Thing is, they can't locate the island. The Royal Australian Navy, the US Navy and our boat all came up short."

"Come on," Jan said. "I'll introduce you to him."

— • ● • —

"Hey Jake," Jan said as she moved through the crowd. "Let me introduce you to Mae."

"Hi," Jake said. "You must be new?"

"Yeah. My mom started a new real estate business here this past summer."

"This is Carson," Jake said as she walked up with the drinks. "Carson, meet Mae."

"You want a drink?" Carson asked. "I brought this for Jake but you're welcome to have it."

"Take it," Jake insisted. "Stubby and I will get a couple more."

"Right, bro," Stubby said. "Let's go."

"Think she could be the one?" Stubby asked as they walked away.

"Could be. Let's find out more about her." *Mae sure asked a lot of questions about me.*

The rest of the evening proved to be uneventful.

Jake and his three friends said their goodbyes and headed to the car.

Jake noticed Mae getting into a white Jeep Wrangler. *Maybe that's her mom.* Walking to the Mustang he made note of the license number intending to pass it on to SSgt. James so that he could check it out.

The mustang pulled out of the parking lot into a warm starry night, great for riding with the top down. The four friends enjoyed the ride to Jan's house. Stubby walked Jan to the door. Jake and Carson got out of Jan's Mustang and into Stubby's back seat again.

"What did you think of Mae," Jake asked matter-of-factly.

"I'd like to know more about her but she seems okay, I guess. She expressed a lot of interest in you. Not that I'm jealous or anything. She gives me the impression she has something on her mind."

Just then Stubby opened his door.

"Hey you two," Stubby said. "Let's get Carson home before the clock strikes 24 hundred hours."

Stubby pulled into Carson's driveway. Jake walked her to the door. They exchanged a friendly hug.

"Maybe I'll see you at school or the beach next week," Jake said. "We switch to one-a-day practices. More time for the beach."

"My cheer schedule eases a little too. So, definitely more beach time. It'd be great to see you."

Carson leaned in and gave Jake a light kiss on the cheek and retreated through the front door.

Stubby smiled at Jake when he got back into the car.

"What?" Jake asked.

"I saw Carson kiss you on your cheek. She likes you."

"She's a good friend."

"I'm a good friend. Your best friend. But I don't kiss you on your cheek."

"Come on. It's not like that. Let's go home."

———•●•———

Stubby pulled into Jake's driveway. "Are we going surfing tomorrow?"

"Planning on it," Jake said. "I'll drive. The boards fit better in my pick-up. You want to go early or mid-day?"

"I like to sleep in on Saturday. How about if we go mid-day?"

"I'll come by after lunch and pick you up. See you then."

Jake closed Stubby's car door and slapped the roof, letting Stubby know he could go. They both picked up that signal while crewing on the Legacy. They learned a lot on that boat. He learned a lot during his two week overboard adventure. It all came back to him with a flood of emotion.

"Remember." Jake heard it again.

Chapter Twenty-two

Jake woke up to a clear and sunny Hawaiian Saturday. He and Stubby went to the MCBH beach to surf since not as many people would be there compared to the Kaneohe public beach. Early afternoon and the heat of the day made for a sparse beach population. A few boards dotted the surf. Jake and Stubby paddled out beyond the natural breakwater of the cove.

"The smaller surf will do" Jake said. "It'll help get the kinks out without burying us."

"Speaking of which, here comes one now." Stubby said. "Let's go."

Both boys caught the wave along with a third surfer. All three rode it with ease. All three bailed as the wave died and they paddled back out.

"Hey, nice ride." Jake yelled to the other surfer paddling toward her. "I'm Jake," he said. "You must be new here. I don't think I've seen you before."

"I'm Sue Lyn," the girl said. "I've been surfing along the coastline all morning. This bay seems like a nice area."

"It is. Part of MCBH. There are signs on both sides of the opening. You probably missed them."

"So, we gabbing or surfing?" Stubby asked,

paddling up to the two. "The surf's picking up. We're in for some good waves."

"Like this one," Jake said turning his board to position it for a ride.

Sue Lyn and Stubby followed suit and the three were riding another wave together. All three bailed as the wave flattened out and they paddled back out. Jake noticed a pod of dolphins swimming by. They looked familiar to him. *Could those be the dolphins from the island?* Then the biggest wave of the day came in.

"Here comes a big one," Jake yelled positioning himself to ride it in.

He paddled hard and got up on the wave. Out of the corner of his eye he noticed Sue Lyn try for the same wave and fall.

"Jake, look out," he heard Stubby yell.

Something hit him on the back of the head knocking him off his board, then darkness.

———•●•———

Jake looked down on himself floating in the water. *That's a familiar sight. I bet Ace had the two dolphins next to me to keep me from sinking.*

"Sue's surfboard hit you on the back of the head and knocked you for a loop," Mic said. "When you didn't resurface Stubby dove underwater to look for you. He surfaced for a breath and eyed Sue Lyn. He yelled to her to help him find you, thinking you must be hurt. Sue Lyn gave Stubby a wave and he went under to continue searching. We've been keeping a watchful eye on you. Remember, we're here to assist and inform."

"Hey Mic, it's been a while," Jake said.

"We never left you," Mic said. "Remember your mission to help others be on the new earth with all the saints when Jesus returns."

"Ok. But how come no one could find the island and rescue the Taylors?"

"That will happen in the Lord's time. Remember, He directs His plan."

"Yeah, remember whose you are," Cal chimed in.

As Jake talked with the angels, the peacefulness returned to Jake like he had experienced before. He didn't have answers to his questions, but he knew the Lord watched over him and the Taylors.

— • ● • —

Jake woke up on the beach looking at a wide-eyed Stubby.

"Man, I didn't know what was going on," Stubby said. "That girl's board hit you and you disappeared. I dove under trying to find you. She took off on her board back out of the bay. Then I see a couple of dolphins floating you into shore. I got here in time to pull you up out of the water and on to the beach. And now here we are. You okay?"

"The board bouncing off the back of my head knocked me out. Then, believe it or not, I found myself up above looking down on things unfolding, and my three angels where there."

"The three from your vision?"

"The same three. They reminded me that they always watch over me. Ace had the dolphins support me and float me to shore. Mic also reminded me that I should try and help people be with me on the new earth when Jesus comes back."

"So, how do you do that?"

"Jesus is real," Jake said. "He loves us. That's my word to share with you and anyone else because He's coming back."

"When?"

"I don't know. It doesn't matter. Just know He is and I want you to be with me on the new earth with Him when He does."

"You sure you didn't just get a bump on the head and dream all of this?"

"Did you see the dolphins?"

"Oh, yeah."

"Enough said."

— • ● • —

"I don't think you should drive after that bump on the head," Stubby said, grabbing Jake's keys. "So, who was that mysterious girl out there with us?"

"Her name is Sue Lin. She spent the morning surfing along the coast wherever she found waves. She ended up outside of the bay. She missed the MCBH signs."

"She must be new to Hawaii," Stubby said. "Do you think we'll see her in school. Maybe she's the one we're looking for."

"That would make two possible suspects. I guess we'll see when we get back to classes."

"Classes start on Tuesday next week, right?" Stubby asked.

"Yep. Then we'll get the lay of the land and see how many other non-Marine brat new girls there are."

"Plus, we'll see our two suspects and can watch what they're up to," Stubby said.

"Mae Ling and Sue Lin are our two prime suspects," Jake said. "But let's keep our eyes open for others. We don't want to miss someone else because of our focus on them."

Stubby pulled up into Jake's driveway.

"Here we are, Bro," Stubby said. "I'll jog home from here. You can drop my board off whenever you're up and out. You should lay low for a bit with that bump on the head."

"I will. And yes, I'll tell my mom I got hit in the head by a wild surfboard."

Stubby laughed, slapped Jake on the back and took off. Jake went inside and found his mom on the lanai reading.

"Hey Mom."

"Hi. How was surfing?"

"Interesting."

"Oh, how so?"

"The interesting part began when I got hit on the back of my head by a surfboard. And I'm fine by the way."

"Come here and let me look at your eyes."

Jake walked to his mom and looked her square in the eyes.

"See," Jake said.

After a beat, Jake continued. "I must have been knocked out for a moment or something because I found myself up above looking down on myself in the water. I talked with my three angels. One of them, Ace, directed a couple of dolphins to float me into shore. We talked about our prior time together and they reminded me of my mission for the Lord. I woke up on the beach looking up at Stubby. He'd pulled me up out of the water."

"Are you sure you're alright? Maybe I should take you to the ER."

"Mom, what'll they do that you can't do here and now? Take my blood pressure, watch my eye dilation, monitor me, that's all in your wheelhouse."

"Okay. You're right."

"Besides, except for a bump on the back of my head, I feel fine."

"You take it easy for the rest of the day, and I'll see how you are in the morning."

"I'd like to go to church with you tomorrow," Jake said. "That won't throw Padre for a loop, will it? I mean, I haven't been there in a while."

"You really want to go? What brought this on?"

"You haven't been paying attention Mom. Jesus loves me. He wants me to share what I know about Him."

"Well, I never thought I'd hear those words come out of your mouth. It makes me happy to hear you talk that way. But how?"

"The angels, Sandy, and Jesus Himself convinced me on the island. I intend to follow the teachings of Jesus. You and Padre will have to help me with that, cause I don't know what it all means."

A tear in the corner of his mom's eye got his attention. She had a smile that he hadn't seen since before his dad passed. *If this is what a relationship with Jesus is all about, I want more.*

Jake's phone rang. "Stubby" popped up on the screen.

"Hey, Bro," Stubby said. "Just calling to see how you're doing."

"I'm fine. Mom's keeping a watchful eye on me. She wants me to lay low this afternoon and evening."

"I figured as much."

"Hey. How'd you like to go to church tomorrow morning with my mom and me at the base chapel?"

"What! Who are you and where have you taken my friend Jake?"

"Stubby, I love you like a brother, and this is something I want you to do with me. How about it?"

"Well, okay. I have to say I didn't see that coming. But I guess it fits with everything else that's been happening to you."

"Great! We'll see you in the morning about 0930."

"Sounds like a plan. I have to tell you I can't remember the last time I went to church."

———— • ● • ————

Jake had forgotten about the beauty of the base chapel with its stained-glass windows and contemporary wood trim.

"I hope the roof doesn't cave in on us or that God doesn't strike us dead for being here," Stubby said.

"Come on," Jake said. "He's not like that. As a matter of fact, I can tell you that His angels celebrate us being here, and He's tickled pink."

"I agree with Jake," Karen said smiling at him. "I'm happy both of you came with me this morning."

Looking around, Jake spotted Carson and her family and Jan and her family too. *Shouldn't surprise me.*

The opening hymn brought Sandy front and center in Jake's mind. They sang the one she had sung on the island, *Beautiful Savior.* Chaplain Evans' sermon on prayer said a lot of what Sandy had shared too. Jake noted that Stubby paid attention as well. *This is a great day in the Lord.*

"Stubby, what did you think?" Jake asked after the service. "Sandy told me the same thing Padre said about prayer being like talking with your dad only better. We can talk directly with our heavenly Father because of Jesus."

"I don't know. I'll think about it."

"Good. Cause I want you to be with me on the new earth when Jesus comes back. Remember, that's what the Bible reading talked about."

"There ya go, talking about stuff I don't get."

"You will. We'll talk more another time."

"I welcome you both to attend with me every Sunday," Karen said. "Weekly worship teaches us a lot, but your presence helps you receive it."

Chapter Twenty-three

Jake heard the bell urging kids to be in their classrooms like an alarm clock with no snooze button ringing. The jammed hallways emptied and became quiet. Closed lockers meant silence reigned again. A new school year began.

He sat across from Stubby in first period precalculus. Surveying the other kids he didn't notice any newbies in the class, only math whizzes.

Second hour English Lit was a whole different story. He and Stubby found desks near Carson and Jan and Sheila. He spotted Mae sitting near the front and Sue sitting in the back row on the far side.

This will be interesting. He caught Stubby's eyes and nodded his head toward Sue. "Remember her from surfing on Saturday? Her board gave me the header."

"Yeah, that's her. She did quite the disappearing act."

Stubby started sharing the story with Jan and Carson but the bell rang to start class so they agreed to meet up for lunch and finish the story.

After class ended Jake and Stubby got up to leave.

"Hey, it's Jake right," Sue said coming up from behind them. "You don't look any worse for wear."

"No thanks to you," Stubby said. "Where did you disappear to?"

"By the time I got my board, you had a bead on Jake. So, I paddled back to the beach where I parked and called it a day. Besides, I didn't want to come into a beach where I'm not authorized to be."

"Under the circumstances it probably would've been okay," Jake said.

"Well, I didn't want to take any chances. I'm new to the island."

The third hour bell began to ring and the kids scattered for their classrooms. Jake grabbed Stubby and they headed for their study hall. They found Carson and Jan there and sat with them.

"I saw the new girl, Sue, talking with you guys," Jan said. "What did she have to say?"

"We kind of bumped into her Saturday afternoon," Jake said. "Stubby and I were surfing in the bay and she came in from the ocean side on her board. She told me her name was Sue Lyn. Then a wave came and we were off."

"We paddled back out," Stubby said. "I paddled over to join in the conversation with Jake and her when another big wave came in and away we went again. This time Sue bailed. Her board went flying into Jake and knocked him off his board and into the surf. I finally caught sight of him being floated to shore by two dolphins. I've never seen anything like it."

"I must have been knocked out," Jake said. "I had another out of body experience. From up above I looked down at myself and my three angel buddies joined me. We talked for a bit. I woke up on the beach looking up at Stubby."

"Wait a minute," Carson said. "You've had other experiences like this, angels and all?"

"Yeah. I went overboard off the Legacy this summer and I ended up on an island for eight days. It supplied food and water and an amazing girl named Sandy. I met with the three angels several times. I even saw heaven and Jesus through a shimmering crease or doorway in the sky."

"Are you sure that bump on the head didn't knock you a little loopy?" Jan asked.

"No, I'm fine. It was all real. Angels, heaven and Jesus are real."

"Ask him about Sandy," Stubby said with a grin.

"Sandy?" Carson asked.

"She and her dad were shipwrecked on the island with me. After the crew of the Seahawk rescued me we couldn't locate the island. Their maps don't show an island there. The Taylors still need to be rescued. Chaplain Evans keeps that in front of the CO's of the Pacific fleet along with the location where I was found."

"So, tell me about Sandy," Carson said.

"She's pretty cool. She knows survival stuff, swims as good as me and cooks over an open fire. She follows the teachings of Jesus and helped me understand my connection with Him and the angels."

"I remember you saying she was a good-looking Aussie," Stubby said smiling even more. "Equally important you said her dad stood six foot six. Quite the big dude."

Carson smiled at Jake and said, "I'm glad they took such good care of you."

"If they exist," Jan chimed in. "Could be you were

just delirious.”

“No, they're real,” Stubby said. “I believe him and what he says happened. The two dolphins floating him into shore on Saturday prove it. Even got me to church with him and his mom yesterday.”

“Yeah!” both girls said at the same time. “We saw.”

Jake laughed and said, “I thought Padre had a great message. I especially liked the Bible readings about heaven 1.0 and heaven 2.0.”

“Explain that to me again,” Stubby said.

“Sure. When you die your spirit and soul go to heaven with Jesus and others who have died faithful to Him. Your body goes into the ground. It turns to dust. When Jesus comes back the resurrection happens. The faithful dead will be raised and those faithful still alive will be caught up with them to meet Jesus in the sky. Then the earth will be changed in a flash, in the twinkling of an eye, the Bible says. So, there will be a new heaven and a new earth where we will live with Jesus forever. Paradise. Heaven 2.0.”

“I don't think I've heard it put that way before,” Carson said.

“Me either,” Jan said.

“Well, you heard Padre preach about it yesterday,” Stubby said. “The Bible reading talked about it too.”

“All I know is heaven is real,” Jake said. “Jesus is real. He wants all of us to be with Him on the new earth. Just believe Jesus died for you as payment for your sin. His resurrection verifies that. Pass it on.”

The fourth hour bell started to ring and the kids scattered again. Jake and Stubby walked into the chemistry room and sat at a table admiring all the equipment. The lab came equipped with the desired chem paraphernalia.

"This looks like it might be fun," Jake said.

Stubby elbowed him and nodded toward the door. Mae appeared with another newbie. The two of them sat at the table in front of Stubby and Jake.

"Hi," Mae said. "I missed talking with you after English Lit. How's it going?"

"It's all good," Jake said. "Who's your friend?"

"Oh, let me introduce Jun. She moved here from Taiwan this summer. Her dad works in the import/export business."

"Hi guys," Jun said. "Nice to meet you."

"Good to meet you too," Jake said.

"Yeah," Stubby said. "Not many girls take chemistry. Nice to have you here."

"Jun is a chem wiz," Mae said. "I'm going to depend on her to get me through it."

"Did you know Jun before?" Stubby asked.

"No. We met this summer. But she told me she loves chemistry, so I thought what the heck."

"Good to know," Jake said. "This will probably be our toughest course this semester."

"Oh, I'm scared of the precalculus," Mae said. "Math's hard for me."

"Not to worry," Jake said. "Stubby or I can help you with that. Math's our thing."

"Speak for yourself," Stubby said. "I get math but I'm not sure I'd call it my thing."

"Let me put my number in your contacts, in case you want my help," Jake said.

The bell rang and class began. The remainder of the school day proved uneventful. A typical hot and muggy football practice capped off the day.

"Let's head for the bay and a cool down swim," Stubby said. "And of course I mean by way of a burger and fries."

"I'm in," Jake said. "On the way we can talk about our three spy girl suspects."

Stubby maneuvered his car toward food, and MCBH and the beach. "By my count, we have three suspects, any of whom could be our spy."

"I agree" Jake said. "Could be any of the three."

"I think we should give their names to SSgt. James," Stubby said. He can do a background check on them. Might make quick work of this whole spy thing."

"Good idea. I'll call him tonight. For now, let's eat and go to the beach. We might find the girls there and the water will feel great post-practice."

Stubby pulled into the beach parking lot and found a spot near Jan's Mustang. Walking through the tall grass and down the slope to the beach, Jake spied Carson with dripping wet hair sitting on a blanket with Jan.

"Hey you two," he yelled. "The water good?"

"Great," Carson said. "Practice?"

"Hot," Stubby said. "We came here to cool down. Speaking of which, last one in's a rotten egg!"

He sprinted to the water with Jake right behind him. They both dove headfirst into the surf.

"This feels so good," Jake yelled to Stubby.

Fifteen minutes of swimming cooled Jake down but made him even more tired. He and Stubby body surfed into the shore and sat down with the girls.

"Well, one day of school down and one hundred and seventy-nine to go," Stubby said.

"It was great catching up with everyone again," Jan said. "Lot's of new kids whose parents came PCS (permanent change of station) over the summer."

"Lot's of kids gone too," Carson said. "Hopefully, the four of us will be able to stay here for the year."

"I'm not going anywhere anytime soon," Jake said. "Except maybe out of base housing. My mom's got a good job at the base hospital and lots of friends here. Even her special friend, Padre Evans. They're good together."

"My dad's been here forever," Stubby said. "I've heard him talk about retiring here at some point."

"You've been a good friend these past years," Jake said. "And you two girls got here two years ago in time to help me through the loss of my dad. One more year and your dads will be in the rotation window."

"Let's not worry about that now," Carson said. "We've got a year to enjoy each other's friendship."

"Carson, the ever optimistic one," Stubby said. "I'm the ever hungry one so Jake, let's git. Time to get home for supper."

"See you tomorrow," Jake said, getting up and brushing off the sand.

"See you tomorrow," Jan and Carson said in unison.

Chapter Twenty-four

"Hi sweetie," **Karen** said when Jake came through the door. "Supper's ready in ten minutes. Did your first day of school go well?"

"Hi Mom. School was okay. After practice Stubby and I went to the beach for a swim. We met Jan and Carson there. I'm full of sand so I'm going to take a quick shower before we eat."

Jake showered and dressed. He picked up his phone and noticed he'd missed a call. He didn't recognize the number but there was a message.

"Hi Jake. It's Mae from chem. I know it's only been one class, but I need some help with math. Please call me at this number. Thanks. Bye."

That's interesting. We didn't really do anything today. I wonder what she really wants.

Jake and Karen enjoyed a supper of mahi mahi, baked potatoes, and salad with fresh pineapple on the side. They both shared the highlights of their day. Jake volunteered to do the dishes. He put them in the dishwasher and made his lunch for school.

"I'll be in my room studying, mom," he said as he left the kitchen.

"Hey SSgt. James," Jake said, answering his cell phone. "Find anything out about the three names I gave you?"

"Nothing popped so far. We're waiting to hear from some other agencies yet. I called to say intel says there's been an uptick in chatter. Could be nothing. Could be something coming. I wanted to give you a heads up."

"Thanks for that. I had a call from Mae, one of the three, asking for some math help. It's a little strange because we didn't really do much yet."

"Keep your eyes and ears open. If you pick up on anything, let me know."

"Ok, I will. Bye."

Jake searched his contacts for Mae's number and pressed the call icon.

"Hi, this is Mae," she answered.

"Hey, Mae. It's Jake returning your call."

"Oh, hi Jake. Yeah, I'm not sure about the math in the reading assignment for tomorrow. I know I'm in a different class section, but I wondered if you could help me with it. I know it's supposed to be review, but I'm not sure I ever got it to begin with."

"Happy to help. Got your book handy?"

"Yeah. It's right here."

"Ok. Let's start with chapter one first page."

He explained the concepts to Mae page by page.

"Tomorrow there'll probably be a pop quiz," Jake said. "No biggy. You should do fine."

"Thanks Jake. I really appreciate this."

"Just remind your friend Jun she said she would help with chemistry. Pretty sure I'll need it."

"I'll tell her. Thanks again. See you tomorrow."

"I'll be there."

Switching off the call, Jake picked up his video game controller and settled in.

———•❂•———

Jake picked up Stubby on his way to school. The day dawned with another beautiful Hawaiian morning complete with sunshine, warm temps and sea salt in the air.

"Hey," Stubby said as he got into Jake's truck. "What a great day. I get to brag about beating you on Playstation last night."

"Don't let it go to your head."

"It doesn't happen that often," Stubby said with a grin. "So, when I beat you I got to make it known."

"Alright, alright. Enjoy."

First hour math was a breeze, quiz and all. I wonder how Mae will do.

"You should be bold and sit by Sue in English Lit," Stubby said. "If she's a possible spy you should try and learn more about her."

"Ok. Then you sit by Mae and get to know her. Divide and conquer."

"Sounds like a plan."

"Hi Sue," Jake said as he took the desk next to hers. "So, your family moved here this past summer."

"Hi Jake. Yeah, we settled in. My dad's meeting his business goals. Hopefully, we'll be staying here a while. We've moved a lot."

"Just you and your dad?"

"My mom died before I turned four. It's been me and my dad since then."

"Where did you move here from?"

"Hey, why all the questions?"

"Oh, I'm sorry. We had a couple of minutes before the bell and I thought I'd try to get to know you better."

"No worries. You like to surf. How about we go surfing together sometime soon. Plenty of time to talk then. I promise not to shoot my board at you again."

"Oh, did you aim it at me the other day then?" Jake asked with a stern tone. "I just thought it accidently hit me."

"The grin on your face tells me you're being sarcastic. It was an accident and I'm sorry."

"No worries, it's cool. How about we go surfing on Saturday? I'll pick you up after lunch and we can go to the MCBH beach. You can come as my guest."

"That sounds fun."

"Here," Jake said handing Sue his phone. Put your address and number in my contacts."

Sue typed in her info and then texted it to herself so she would have Jake's number too.

"Here you go," she said handing the phone back to Jake. "I'm looking forward to Saturday."

Jake looked over at Stubby talking with Mae as the bell rang for class to begin. *He could double up with me on Saturday.*

"How did your conversation with Mae go?" Jake asked Stubby as they walked to their third hour study hall.

"She's pretty cool. I don't think I picked up anything we didn't already know about her. How about

Sue?"

"She's more guarded with info about herself than Mae. I invited her to go surfing Saturday afternoon. You want to double up with us?"

"Sounds like a plan. I'll invite Mae. We'll be able to compare them side by side and see if one of them could be the secret agent we're looking for."

"That's kinda what I thought. Let me know. I'll plan to pick you up after lunch and then we can get the girls."

Arriving at third hour study hall Jake and Stubby sat down with Jan and Carson who sat at a table near the front of the hall.

"Hi guys," Jan said. "How's your day going?"

"It's been interesting," Jake said. "I sat by Sue in English Lit and ended up inviting her to go surfing Saturday afternoon. Stubby's going to double with me."

"I'm going to ask Mae if she would like to go," Stubby said. "It'll give me a chance to get to know more about her."

"How about we meet up with you at the beach," Carson said.

"Great idea," Jake said. "I hoped you'd say that. Stubby and I are on a mission to know more about them. You two can help."

"I've noticed you have an interest in them," Carson said.

"Well, there's a little more to it than that," Jake said. "I can't tell you all the details but we want to learn about non-Marine brat girl newbies in our class."

"That's a pretty specific group," Carson said. "If I didn't know better I'd say you might be looking for something. Care to share?"

"For now," Jake said, "Let's just say we want to find out more about their religious backgrounds."

"Does that have anything to do with your new Jesus thing?" Jan asked.

"Maybe, sort of."

"It's some other stuff too," Stubby said.

"Sounds a bit cryptic," Carson said. "When will you two tell us what the real story is? I know you know more than you've shared."

"For now, we want to get to know them better," Jake said. "Hopefully, we can be friends." *Unless one of them turns out to be the secret agent girl.*

"Ok," Jan said. "We'll plan to meet you all at the K-bay beach on Saturday."

The bell rang, ending third hour and Jake told the girls bye and headed to his fourth hour chem class with Stubby in tow. He found Mae at a table and sat across from her leaving the seat by her for Stubby. *I wonder why Jun's not here.* The uneventful class turned out to be a lecture by their teacher, Mr. Phillips. *There'll be a big assignment soon. I hope not for the weekend.*

Jake joined Stubby for their fifth hour lunch and then eased through the remainder of the school day. He liked that this week's football practice began the prep for the first game a week from Saturday. *Altogether, a nice way to ease back into the school year.*

Chapter Twenty-five

Jake and Stubby pulled up in front of a small Hawaiian bungalow with the address Sue had entered in Jake's cell phone.

"This place looks as sleek as Legacy under full sail," Jake said opening his door. "I'll go up and get Sue. Be right back."

As Jake got out of his truck, Sue came running out of the house. She wore a yellow floral cover-up with her long black hair pulled back in a ponytail. She grabbed her surfboard and met Jake coming up the walk.

"Hi Jake," Sue said as he attempted to take her board. "I got it. Just show me where you want it."

"Put it in the back of my truck with ours. Hope you don't mind. I invited Stubby and Mae to go with us."

"Cool. Did you think you needed protection from me?"

"No. Not at all. More is always better when surfing." *Especially when we're trying to find out if you're a spy or not.*

Jake drove to Mae's address. He stopped in front of a Main Street apartment in town. The street bustled with the normal Saturday afternoon tourist rush. Mae must have been watching for them and came running out. She wore a coverup like Sue's except hers was solid pink. She didn't know how to surf much less have a board. Stubby planned to teach her using his spare board.

Stubby got out and opened the rear door.

"Hey Mae," Stubby said. "You ready to ride the wild surf?"

"I'm ready to learn," Mae said with a tentative smile as she got into the truck.

"Hey Mae," Jake and Sue said in unison.

"Hi you guys. Turned out to be a great day for the water. I'm excited to learn how to surf."

"Easy to do once you get over the fear of falling off into a wave," Sue said. "Probably won't be any big waves today, so that shouldn't be a problem."

"We'll take it nice and easy," Stubby said. "You'll be fine."

Driving into the MCBH beach parking lot, Jake counted more cars than during the week. He spotted Jan's mustang and pulled in next to it.

"Keep an eye out for Jan and Carson," Jake said. "We can put our towels and stuff by them. Not that anyone would take them."

Stubby grabbed his two boards out of the truck bed and handed one to Mae.

"Let me introduce you to the first lesson of surfing," Stubby said. "Carry your board."

Jake and Sue each grabbed their boards and the foursome walked down to the beach. The heat of the day would make the cool ocean water feel good. The light breeze made for a light surf, perfect for teaching a beginner.

"Hey," Jake said, approaching Jan and Carson. "You remember Mae, and this is Sue."

"Hi, Sue," Jan and Carson said.

"Hi. Jake invited me to come surfing with him today. Beautiful day for it. Smaller waves though."

"So, you're new at school this year," Carson said. "Where did you move from?"

"My dad's business keeps us moving," Sue said. "We came here from Shanghai. I told my dad no more moves while I'm in high school. I hope he heard me."

"Nice to meet you," Jan said. "I don't surf, but I love the sun and I like to swim."

"Little Miss Modest," Carson said. "She swims on the school swim team, and we hope she'll take the state title this year."

"Hey, Mae," Stubby said. "Let's go."

Grabbing his board, Stubby nudged Mae to the water and began explaining surfing basics to her.

"Not the biggest waves," Jake said to Sue. "Let's head out and see what we can ride."

"Ok, let's go."

Jake and Sue paddled out from shore and watched for some waves to develop.

"So, you moved around a lot because of your dad's business," Jake said. "Where did you live before Shanghai?"

"We've been all over the Pacific," Sue said. "Before Shanghai we lived in the Philippines. Before that we lived in New Zealand and Australia. Because of my dad's type of business, we always live near port towns. Because of that I love to surf. It's the one thing I can do to take my mind off my problems."

"What kind of problems do you have?"

Sue sighed. "The biggest one is the constant movement and lack of longtime friends. Sometimes the loneliness really gets me down."

"I get that. My dad served as a career Marine. So, we moved every two or three years. Fortunately, we regularly cycled through Kaneohe. It became a home for me. My dad passed a year ago, so my mom and I will probably have to move out of base housing. I don't know what that'll mean."

"So, you understand how I feel," Sue said.

"Yes, I do. But I recently learned that a whole lot more to life exists than where I am or what my circumstances are."

"What do you mean?"

"I mean, this past summer I crewed on a boat and went overboard in a storm. Ten days later a Navy Seahawk rescued me, but I only spent two of the ten days in the water. The other eight days I survived on an island. Some very wild things happened to me. Bottom line, I know Jesus is real. He loves me. He loves you, too. And He wants you and me and everyone to be with Him on the new earth when he comes back. But some don't want to be there."

Sue had a look on her face like she'd seen a crazy person.

"You don't have to believe me," Jake said. "But during those eight days I talked with angels. I saw Jesus on His heavenly throne surrounded by all the faithful who have died. I can guarantee you there is life after this life for all who believe in Him."

"You seem quite convinced about that. I have an Aussie friend who has the same conviction of belief."

"Not just what I saw," Jake said. "I felt it too. I had

a feeling of total peace. When Jesus spoke to me, I knew, I remembered."

Sue still looked at Jake. Then he noticed her looking behind him.

"Turn around," she said, getting her board on track to ride the incoming wave. "Let's ride."

Jake looked over his shoulder while positioning himself for a wave. It wasn't the biggest, but decent enough. Quickly, both got up, riding the wave toward shore. Not awesome in the surfing department but up and riding just the same.

"I call this a passive ride," Sue yelled.

Jake laughed. "Kind of like we ride with God."

Sue shook her head with a look of confusion. Jake noted contemplation reigning for the remainder of the ride.

As the wave began to flatten out, both riders bailed on it. The wave took Jake close to shore and Stubby and Mae.

"We'll go back out with you," Stubby yelled. "Mae's ready to give it a try for real."

Stubby and Mae paddled out to join Jake and Sue.

"Hey you guys," Jan yelled. "Carson and I are coming out too." They dove in and caught up to the surfers. They swam alongside for a while. Then they turned back toward shore and swam to where they could touch bottom.

"We'll watch from here," Carson yelled, bouncing off the bottom.

"You've got it, Mae," Jan said, matching Carson bounce for bounce.

Stubby and Mae positioned themselves for any reasonable wave that would come.

"When I tell you, start paddling toward shore like crazy," Stubby said. "When you feel the wave pushing the board, grab the sides and hold on and just ride this first time. No need to try and stand till you get the feel of wave and board."

"I feel like I'm ready," Mae said. "Tell me when."

"Looks like there's a wave building," Sue said. "Let's spread out and get ready for it. It's not big but it'll do for a starter."

The four surfers were watching intently as the wave moved in.

"Start paddling," Stubby yelled to Mae.

Soon all four were riding it. Three were standing watching Mae up on her knees holding on to the sides of her board.

"Enjoying the ride," Stubby yelled.

"She looks comfortable on her board," Jake chimed in.

Then Mae got her feet under her and stood up. The riders breezed past Jan and Carson who yelled their approval and cheered Mae on.

"That was amazing," Mae shouted as the wave flattened. "Let's do it again."

She turned her board and started paddling back out to catch another.

"Am I good or what?" Stubby said, turning to paddle out with her.

"Either you're a great teacher or Mae's a natural," Jake said, as he and Sue joined them.

"I think a little of both," Sue said.

Jake surfed and swam with his friends well into the afternoon. Soon they all sat on the beach air drying in the hot afternoon Hawaiian sun cooled by the ocean breeze.

— • ● • —

"That was fun," Mae said. "Now I know why surfers love surfing so much."

Jake sighed. "No more Saturday surfing for Stubby and me until football season ends. Our games are all on Saturday afternoons."

"We need to celebrate the day," Stubby said. "I suggest ice cream at Mickey D's."

"Great idea," Jan said.

"Let's go," Jake said. "We can go out the gate up the street from Mickey D's to take the girls home."

"I didn't realize you can get on and off base so easy," Sue said. "I thought there would be a lot more security."

"It depends on the threat level," Jake said. "A higher level brings on more security measures. Most of the gate guards know us, so that helps. When the threat level goes up it means more than vehicle stickers. They start checking ID's and registrations. Guests get limited or turned away."

Jake pulled into Mickey D's followed by Jan and Carson. They parked in the rear and walked inside together. Sheila worked at the register and smiled when she saw them.

"Hey, you guys. Looks like you've been at the beach."

"Stubby taught me how to surf," Mae said. "It was fun."

"She's a natural," Sue said. "I'll be curious to see how she handles bigger waves."

"Yeah, it's kind of flat out there today," Jake said. "But what a great day for a beginner."

They all ordered cones or shakes. Sheila served them. Jake and Stubby picked up the tab.

"That reminds me," Sheila said. "Do you guys know Jun? She's new this year. She came in here a bit ago for lunch. I didn't see anyone with her. She wasn't very talkative either."

Jake looked at Stubby. His eyes reflected the same question Jake had. *How did she get on base unescorted?*

The six found a table and settled in. Jake excused himself to go to the restroom. He called SSgt. James.

"Just a heads up," Jake told him. "One of the three girls I had you check on, Jun, was seen on base this afternoon at McDonalds unescorted."

"Thanks for letting me know. We'll check it out. If you hear or see anything more, let me know."

"Roger that. For what it's worth, she missed school a couple of days at the end of the week."

Jake rejoined his friends and started in on his strawberry shake. Each member of the group shared what they knew about Jun. In the end, Jake didn't learn anything new about her. *Could she be the one?*

Jan and Carson said their goodbyes and left.

"We should get the girls home too," Jake said to Stubby.

"Right you are," Stubby said. "We don't want to be late for supper."

The four piled back into Jake's truck and headed toward the gate and town. Arriving at the gate. there was a line of traffic both ways. A posted sign said, "ID check in progress."

Jake and Stubby pulled out their wallets.

"We're not going to be a problem?" Sue asked.

"No worries," Jake said. "You're our guests." *This gate check is because of my phone call.*

Sue and Mae each pulled out their driver's license and handed them to Jake. The gate guard stepped up to the truck.

"Hi Jake," the guard said. "I need to see your ID's."

Jake pulled his out of his wallet and collected the other three's ID's and gave all four to the guard. He looked them over matching each occupant to the respective ID. He returned them to Jake and waved them through.

"Have a nice day," the guard said.

Jake proceeded through the gate. "The security level must be higher than when we came through earlier." *I know why.*

Jake drove to Mae's first. Stubby walked her up to the door.

"Today was a fun day," Sue said to Jake while they waited for Stubby. "Maybe we can do it again sometime only with bigger waves."

"Count on it," Jake said. "Following up on our conversation from out in the water, how would you like to join me at the base chapel tomorrow morning for worship? I can swing by and pick you up and be your escort onto the base."

"Oh, I don't know. Let me think about it. I'll text you later."

"No pressure. If not tomorrow maybe another time."

Stubby opened the door and jumped in.

"Mae said she enjoyed today so much that she wants to get her own board. I told her she could use mine anytime. She thinks surfing is cool.

Stubby, seeing the look on Jake's face said, "I feel like I interrupted something."

"No worries," Jake said. "I asked Sue if she'd like to go to church tomorrow."

"I told him I'd think about it," Sue chimed in.

"Well, I didn't see that coming," Stubby said with a grin. "But it is a topic of conversation lately."

Jake drove on to Sue's house. When they arrived, Sue grabbed her board and carried it to the door, Jake following.

"I really did enjoy the day," Sue said. "Your friends are cool too."

"Today was a good day. After today I think you could say they're your friends too. Let me know about tomorrow."

"I'll text you," Sue said as she stood her board against the front porch and went inside.

Jake returned to his truck and got in. Stubby had a sheepish grin on his face.

"So, you asked her to go to worship tomorrow," Stubby said. "Seems like you're developing a new habit."

"It's absolutely new. I want all my friends to be with me on the new earth with Jesus when He comes back."

"Wow! Your overboard experience had a way bigger impact on you than I first thought."

"Hey, I saw Jesus for real. He spoke to me. I will never be the same ole Jake. Now I want to share that He wants everyone on the new earth with Him."

Jake heard it in his head again, "Remember."

Chapter Twenty-six

Sandy stared at the colorful sunrise on another beautiful day on her island paradise. Near as she could figure it was Sunday, the Lord's Day. The day found her sitting on the beach following her morning swim complete with dolphin fun. Interacting with the dolphins every day reminded her of Jake.

While she swam, she left her father to complete his daily firewood gathering task. Not a swimmer like Sandy, he liked hiking through the island woods more.

She walked into camp to a full wood pile and fruit for breakfast washed and on the table. Her dad had cleaned up and sat at the table prepping the VHF transmitter. He did a "Mayday" blast at alternate times of the day since she had returned with the Legacy's emergency bag. The solar charger for the batteries worked intermittently at best. That made the process challenging.

Looks like you're ready to do another blast with the transmitter," Sandy said. "It's been weeks since Jake disappeared. Seems like if he was alive, we might have been rescued by now. I remember Jake said when he turned on the GPS it showed our position in the middle of the ocean. Maybe no one's found us because of that."

"This equipment has a limited range," David reminded his daughter. "All we can do is put out a signal and pray some ship sails by close enough to pick it up."

"We'll do it again at noon tomorrow?" Sandy asked.

"That'll depend on how well it recharges. The charger doesn't perform at a level as advertised. But first, it's the Lord's Day, so let's lift Him up in praise and prayer."

Father and daughter sang a favorite hymn together. Sandy read a portion of Luke's gospel. Both offered words of prayer including thanksgiving for their needs being met in the beautiful island setting, hope for Jake's wellbeing and their rescue.

Sandy loved how the time of worship always brought a feeling of peace and calm to her. It helped her remember she belonged to the Lord Jesus. He would take care of them.

———•●•———

Jake and his mom picked up Stubby and drove to the base chapel for Sunday worship.

"Sue texted me last night and said she'd have to pass on worship today," Jake said. "But maybe another time."

"I kinda think you'll hold her to it," Stubby said. "We have lots of other prospects too. And don't forget we need to get to know all the new non-marine brats in our class."

"All true," Jake said, pulling into the MCBH

Chapel parking lot.

"Here we are," Karen said. "Chaplain Evans told me he has the message today. I get so much more out of it when he preaches. He's simple, straightforward and to the point."

"Well, let's go hear what he has to say," Stubby said, opening Karen's door for her.

"Coming to the base chapel always calms me," Karen said. "I like the message of the beautiful stained-glass windows behind the altar too."

"Mom, you have an interesting look on your face," Jake said.

"This is my 'I'm at peace with the Lord' look. When I come here on Sunday for worship, I know God is present because of what Jesus did for us. I'm right with God. He's my heavenly Father and one day I'll be with Him forever."

"You get all that from going in and sitting down?" Stubby asked.

"That's right," Karen said. "Every week I experience the same thing. And today is even more special because you and Jake choose to be here with me. Jesus will be here with this family of believers gathered in His Name to worship Him."

"Hi Huber family," Carson said as she and her family sat down behind them. "Hi to you too, Stubby."

"Hi Koke family," the three answered in unison.

Jan and her family slid in behind the Kokes.

Chaplain Evans came up to the front and welcomed everyone and began the worship service saying, "Remembering our baptism, we begin in the Name of the Father and of the Son and of the Holy Spirit. Amen."

Songs of praise, Bible readings and prayer set the tone for a message by Padre. He shared words that truly hit home with Jake about the Father, His Son Jesus and heaven. He said that God forgives sinners because of Jesus' death and resurrection. He also reminded everyone that Jesus was coming back just like the apostles watched him go.

Jake remembered his conversations with the three angels. *That's what Mic was talking about. It's when Jesus brings there to here on a new earth.*

Padre spoke more about God's love for all and wanting everyone to be with Him.

"That's a message for all," Padre said. "We have received it and get to share it."

Jake remembered his visit to heaven and the love of Jesus he had felt. Leaning over to Stubby he said, "That's what I'm talking about."

Stubby grinned and said, "Padre says it so I can understand it. But you're more convincing."

Worship ended and people gathered for juice or coffee and donuts. Jake and Stubby met up with Carson and Jan. While they ate donuts and drank POM (pineapple, orange, and mango) juice they shared thoughts about Padre's message.

"This makes two weeks in a row for you boys," Carson said. "Is coming to worship related to your overboard experience?"

"I'm here 'cause Jake insisted I needed to be here with him," Stubby said. "Something about being on a new earth with him and Jesus. Now that I think about it, Padre's message talked about that too."

"I'm glad you see the connection," Jake said. "Coming to worship helps me remember my experience from the island and what I'm to be about. It's what Padre said. Sharing Jesus' love."

"Isn't that what all Christians are supposed to do?" Jan asked.

"Yes, they are," Jake said. "But their head belief gets cluttered and in the way of their hearts. I'm going to follow the teachings of Jesus and let people around me know about His love. People need to know He's coming back and wants to have them on the new earth with me and Him."

"You talked about that new earth thing last week," Jan said. "I never really thought about heaven on earth."

"A lot of faithful people believe that when they die, they'll go to heaven and be with Jesus, which is true," Jake said. "Unfortunately, that's as far as they go. That's heaven 1.0. When Jesus returns, the resurrection happens and the earth is changed. It's heaven to the max, 2.0. I don't know much about the in-between time."

"I think you're right that most Christians don't think about life after the resurrection and Jesus' return," Carson said. "What about all of our friends who don't even know Jesus?"

"Exactly," Jake said. "Those of us who know can invite those who don't to be on the new earth, or heaven, with us. Padre said it in his message."

"Do I hear you kids talking about me," Chaplain Evans said, approaching the table where they sat.

"Hey Padre," Stubby said. "We were talking about your message today. I think it complements what Jake learned during his island experience."

"The complement would be that teenagers are

talking about my message at all," Chaplain Evans said with a smile. "Putting that together with Jake's experience this past summer intrigues me. Even more interesting today is the message traffic that I received from the Roosevelt. There's been some VHF radio chatter picked up near where they rescued you, Jake. That's all I know."

Chaplain Evans walked away to meet with others who had stayed for a bit after worship. His words left Jake wondering if somehow the Taylors could be involved with the radio signals.

"This has definitely been an interesting morning," Stubby said. "While this little snack tasted good, I'm ready for brunch. How about it?"

"Mom and I usually go to the Officer's Club brunch," Jake said. "I know Stubby'll go with us since I'm his ride."

"My mom's got a roast in the slow cooker," Carson said.

"Yeah, my dad plans on grilling today," Jan said. "See you both at school tomorrow."

Jake, Stubby and Karen said their goodbyes and went off to Sunday brunch at the O'Club.

— • ● • —

Jake recognized Commander Looker, XO of the USS Roosevelt, walking by their table.

"Hey Commander," Jake said, standing up to greet him.

"Hi, Jake." Commander Looker said.

"This is my mom, Karen, and my best friend, Stubby.

"Good to finally meet you Karen," Commander Looker said, extending his hand. "I feel like I know you from Jake's adventure. I'm glad I get to meet you in person."

Karen shook his hand. "I'm glad to meet you too, Commander. Thanks for taking care of my son. Everyone on the Roosevelt has been kind and helpful to me. I can't thank you enough."

"Karen, please call me John. I'm proud of my crew. They're happy to serve."

"I didn't think the Roosevelt was due in port yet," Jake said.

"No, the Roosevelt's not back. I flew in on a COD for a pre-return meeting tomorrow. But I'm glad I ran into you. I think you'll be interested to know that we picked up some more faint 'Mayday' signals. They're sporadic and we haven't been able to pin down a position. It seems to be coming from a general area a little east of where we rescued you. We informed the Australian authorities who began another search and rescue operation. The signal could be from the Taylors and the island you stayed on."

"Wow," Stubby said slapping Jake on the back. "That's some news! By that grin on your face, you must be happy to hear it."

"I pray they can be found," Karen said. "I know how happy that would make Jake."

Jake finally found his voice and said, "Chaplain Evans mentioned this morning that he'd heard some chatter. But this is great news XO. Any way I can get in on updates?"

"I can make sure that Chaplain Evans gets any message traffic about it. He would be your best point of contact."

"Thanks. That means a lot."

"I see my group has arrived, so I'll say goodbye. Stubby, good to meet you. Jake, I have a feeling our paths will cross again."

"Fair winds and following seas, XO," Jake said shaking the XO's hand.

The XO nodded and joined his group.

Jake, Stubby and Karen went through the buffet line and returned to their table.

"He's a very nice man," Karen said. "And he's been very helpful."

"If it hadn't been for him and Captain Hardy I might not have been found," Jake said. "The faint 'Maydays' being heard are the Taylors. I'm sure of it. I'll keep talking with God about that."

"On that note, let's thank Him for this wonderful food," Karen said.

"Let's do that and dig in," a smiling Stubby said.

Karen shared words of thanks and all enjoyed a tasty brunch.

After they dropped Stubby at his house, Karen said, "I invited Chaplain Evans to join us for supper this evening."

"That's great, Mom," Jake said. "I can talk with him some more about the mayday chatter."

"I know your hopes are up about the Taylors being rescued. Just remember it will happen in the Lord's time. Be patient, dear."

"Yeah, I know Mom. I just wish I could do more."

"Keeping them before the Lord in prayer is the most important thing you can do. Trust Him with the details."

"You're preaching to the choir, mom."

"I'm so happy you learned to sing," Karen said, hugging her son.

"I've got some homework to get done. Let me know when Padre gets here."

"I will, honey."

Jake spent time reviewing his math and working on chemistry. He opened his lit book when his phone rang.

"Hi, Mae, what's happening?"

"Hi, Jake. I need some help with tomorrow's math assignment. Are you free?"

"Sure thing," Jake said.

Jake walked Mae through the main points of the assignment, explaining when she didn't understand.

"You make it so easy. Thanks for your help."

"Happy to do it."

"I've been trying to call Jun all afternoon for some chem help," Mae said. "Her phone goes right to voicemail. I hope everything is okay."

"Sheila said she saw her yesterday at Mickey D's," Jake reminded her. "How well do you know her?"

"Not very well. We've talked a few times around classes. But that's all. Thanks again for the help, Jake. I'll see ya tomorrow."

"Ok. See ya tomorrow."

Jake pushed the 'end call' button on his cell. *Could Jun be caught up in something.*

Chapter Twenty-seven

"Jake," Karen called out from the front of the house. "Chaplain Evans just pulled in the driveway."

"Ok, Mom. Be there in a minute."

Jake heard the doorbell ring. He went into the living room. Karen opened the front door to the man they'd known for many years as Padre. He served as the chaplain who'd helped them deal with his dad's death over a year ago. Now he was a friend, Jim.

"Hi, Jim," Karen said. "Come in."

"Hi, Karen. Here, I brought this to go with supper," Jim said offering a bottle of pinot grigio.

"That's my favorite," Karen said. "It'll go great with the fish we're having for supper. I'll put it in the fridge. Please have a seat."

Karen went into the kitchen. Jim sat in the living room with Jake.

"Hey, Padre."

"Hi Jake. I have to say, I always feel at home when I visit here. Probably because it isn't just a house. It's a comfy mix of Marine, American and Hawaiian with the Lord's blessing over it all. It's a home."

"I agree," Jake said. "How's your day been?"

"The Lord's Day is always a good day, Jake. How

about you?”

“Today has been interesting. You’ll never guess who we ran into at brunch today. Commander Looker came by our table. I introduced him to mom and Stubby. He told me about the faint ‘Mayday’ calls they picked up on the Roosevelt. He said they seem to be coming from an area a little east of where the Seahawk rescued me. I think it could be the Taylors.”

“That matches what I’ve been hearing from several sources. I’ve been keeping the whole situation in my prayers.”

“Commander Looker said he would hook you to the message traffic about it,” Jake said. “So, if you hear anything more, please let me know.”

“Sure thing, Jake.”

“Oh, one more thing, Padre. Have you heard of anyone being detained on base for security reasons yesterday or today?”

“Odd question,” Padre said. “Why do you ask?”

“Well, you have a high security clearance, right?”

“It’s high enough, Jake. Why?”

“When I got back from my summer crewing school, base security asked me to help identify a female Asian spy posing as a high school junior. With Stubby’s help we identified three possibilities, and I gave their names to SSgt. James. Yesterday, one of the three turned up on base with no apparent escort. She’d also been absent from school the last couple of days. I called and shared that with SSgt. James yesterday afternoon. The two other possibilities came with Stubby and me surfing yesterday afternoon. When we went through the gate to take the girls home, an ID check was underway. I think that happened because of my call. One of the girls, Mae, told me she'd been trying to call Jun, she's the girl, but the call kept going straight to voicemail. That's why I asked."

"I can affirm that base security detained two people last night," Padre said. "More than that you'll need to talk with SSgt. James, since he involved you in it. Call it following the chain of command."

"Okay, I'll call him later."

"Dinner is served," Karen called from the kitchen.

Jake and Chaplain Evans joined Karen around the table.

"It looks and smells great as always," Jake said.

"Jim, would you say grace for us?" Karen asked.

Padre prayed and they enjoyed a pleasant meal and conversation.

Chapter Twenty-eight

Jake went out to sit on the lanai and relax. Pulling out his cell, he called SSgt. James.

"Yes, Jake, we did apprehend the Asian infiltrator and her handler," SSgt. James said. "I thought I would call you tomorrow and let you know. We caught them before any damage was done to the communication network. So, you've completed your mission with your country's thanks."

"It was Jun, wasn't it?" Jake asked.

"Yes, we took her into custody. The interesting twist is that she worked with a civilian employed on base. That's how she got access through the gate. The fact that your friend noticed her, and you called me with the info proved to be just plain lucky."

"Call it a God thing."

"Call it what you want. We caught them in the lock down and ID check. They were practicing a dry run so no harm no foul. We arrested her for illegal entry and false ID. After lengthy conversation she said if we granted her asylum, she would answer all our questions and tell us everything she knew. Her handler won't be so fortunate."

"I'm glad that's done. And I made two new friends

out of it, Mae and Sue."

"You can always find a silver lining."

"Is it okay if I tell Stubby about all this?"

"Sure, just tell him to keep a lid on it."

"Copy that. What about school friends who knew Jun?"

"Listen Jake, less is more. Just tell them in general terms she was detained by base security and you don't know if she'll be back in school or not. That's a true statement because at this point we don't know."

"Okay, thanks SSgt. I'm glad I could help."

"So am I Jake. Stay cool."

Ending the call with SSgt. James, Jake called Stubby.

"Hey," Stubby said. "What's happening?"

"I just talked with SSgt. James. Base security picked up the Asian agent. Turns out it was Jun."

"I'm glad they got her," Stubby said. "I'm even more glad it wasn't Mae or Sue."

"Me too."

"What are we telling kids at school?"

"SSgt. James said just to tell them base security detained her and we don't know if she'll be back to school."

"Well, there ya go. Case closed. Now we can focus on Saturday's football game. Remember, we play football?"

"Yeah, yeah. I remember."

At that exact moment Jake felt a tingle up and down his spine. *What's that all about?* He paused for a beat, told Stubby goodbye and ended the call. Feeling tired, he decided a good night's sleep was what he needed.

"Good night, Mom. I'm going to bed," Jake called out.

"Good night. Sleep well," Jake heard his mom say.

He laid down, closed his eyes and quickly fell asleep.

———•●•———

Jake recognized himself below in bed. He heard a familiar voice.

"Jake," Mic said. "Much has happened and more is to come."

"Hey, Mic. Happy to see you, but what are you talking about?"

"Remembering will keep you safe and see you through," Mic said.

"Remembering what?" Jake asked. "See me through what?"

"He said, 'Remember, you are mine,'" Mic said. "That brings love and peace for you, and for you to share. But Luce seeks otherwise. He would have you forget."

"Remember whose you are, where you are, and what you can do," Ace said.

"Leave the details to Him," Cal said.

Jaked laughed. "You three don't let up. Don't worry I remember it all. I especially remember where I left Sandy and her dad. They need to be rescued. Can you help them?"

"He knows and He can. And He will," Mic said. "When He will."

"Leave your cares with Him and rest," Ace said.

Chapter Twenty-nine

The warmth of a beautiful Hawaiian sunrise greeted Jake and ushered in Monday morning and a new school week. He picked up Stubby and they rode to school in silence. Arriving at the high school they found students all abuzz with excitement anticipating the football home opener on Saturday.

"We're varsity football players," Stubby said smiling from ear to ear. "Practice this week will be all about Saturday's game. I hope you can contain yourself better than you have so far today."

"I'm sorry. After I hung up last night, my mind went to Sandy and her dad. I should tell you I also had a visit with my angel buds."

"No wonder you're so quiet. What did they have to say?"

"I don't know. They always talk in such cryptic terms. Something about remembering God so that I'm not tempted to forget Him. That He can and will rescue Sandy and her dad. Just leave it to Him."

"Good advice. Let's focus that brain power of yours on football. This should be our breakout year, remember."

Jake laughed. "Yeah, I remember. You as wide

receiver/safety and me as fullback/cornerback."

They arrived at their lockers in the middle of the morning chaos. Jake found a paper taped to his locker door. The note from the school's guidance counselor, Ms. Singleton, said, "Please come and see me during your third hour study hall. I need to talk with you about the application process for the Military Service Academies."

Jake showed the note to Stubby.

"You want to come with me?" Jake asked. "Applying doesn't mean you have to go."

"Sure. I'll check it out with you. Besides football and schoolwork, we've got nothing else to do."

Jake and Stubby went to their first hour math class. The bell rang just as they sat down. Jan and Carson looked up from their conversation with Sue. Jake tipped his head and smiled at them. Both smiled back and another school day began.

After math and lit class, Jake found Stubby and they headed to the Guidance office. Ms. Singleton signaled for them to come in.

"Hi boys, have a seat."

The boys sat in chairs across from her desk. Jake took note of her academic credentials hanging on the wall. She had a bookshelf full of college catalogues and a variety of career opportunities.

"I thought Stubby might come with you, Jake. I think the two of you have what it takes to qualify for an appointment to any of the service academies. You have the smarts, good grades and physicality to excel at any one of them. The beginning of your junior year is the perfect time to become familiar with the application process and organize a timeline to get it done. I will tell you the process is much more rigorous than for other schools. You'll have to stay on top of it. Over the next few days, I want you to go to the academy admissions website and look it over and we can talk again. How about the same time next Monday?"

"Okay, Ms. Singleton," Jake said. "I'll take a look and see you next week."

"Me too," Stubby said. "I'm interested enough to check it out. Should I tag along with Jake next Monday?"

"Absolutely. I'll see you both next Monday, third hour."

"Thanks, Ms. Singleton," Jake said.

Stubby echoed Jake's words.

"The Air Force Academy is one of the routes to becoming an officer in the U.S. Space Force," Jake said to Stubby, walking to study hall. "That's what I want to do and where I want to serve."

"I don't have a clue what I want to do," Stubby said. "USAFA (United States Air Force Academy) seems like a possibility, so I might as well start the application process."

Jake laughed and slapped Stubby on the back. They arrived at study hall for the remainder of third hour. They sat down at a table with Jan and Carson and shared about their visit with Ms. Singleton.

"I want to be a nurse or a PA (physician's assistant)," Carson said. "I just don't know about going to an academy. After graduation there's a four-year commitment to active duty."

"College is paid for," Jan said. "So, four years of service isn't a terrible trade off."

"If you want to serve in the military, it becomes a

moot point," Jake said. "I want to serve in the Space Force, so USAFA is the way I think I want to go to get there."

"Must be nice to know what you want to do," Stubby said. "I'll figure it out one of these days."

"Me too," Jan said.

The bell rang and students were off to fourth hour classes. Jake and Stubby headed to chemistry. Entering the chem room, they sat with Mae at her table. That left the empty seat that Jun had occupied.

"I still haven't heard back from Jun," Mae said. "I wonder what's up with her?"

"A friend of mine who works in base security told me they detained her on Saturday and couldn't say whether or not she'd be back at school," Jake said.

"Oh my," Mae said looking concerned. "That doesn't sound good."

"Not good at all," Stubby echoed.

The bell rang and chem class began. The periodic table soon gave way to lunch, US History, PE, physics and finally football practice.

Jake enjoyed practice. He considered it the fun but grueling part of the day. Today's practice started the focused preparation for the team's Saturday game. They would be playing against their cross-island rival. The encounter always promised a higher level of intensity by both players and spectators. Jake knew the drill. His coach would have the team ready. A pep rally on Friday afternoon would get the kids pumped up for Saturday. It would be a fun day.

Jake took Stubby straight home after practice. Even though hungry, Stubby suggested they should forgo getting a snack somewhere because his mom was making a special meal for his dad's birthday. Jake dropped Stubby off. Instead of going home he went to the base chapel to see Chaplain Evans.

He walked into the chapel offices and greeted RP1 Owens.

"Hi, Jake. What can I do for you on this fine Navy Day?"

"Hi, RP1. I'm looking for Chaplain Evans. Is he here?"

"He went home to grab his 'go' bag. He's flying out with Commander Looker on a COD back to the Roosevelt to investigate a chaplain incident. He said he would be stopping by here on his way to the airfield. I expect him any time. Have a seat. I'll text him that you want to see him."

Just then the door opened and in walked Chaplain Evans.

"Hello Jake," Chaplain Evans said. "What brings you by?"

"Hi, Padre. I had some time and thought I'd touch base with you about the Taylors. Have you heard anything more?"

"No, I haven't Jake. But I'm heading to the Roosevelt shortly. If I hear anything new, I'll get word to you. And please give your mom my best."

"Thanks, and I will, Padre. I have this feeling in my gut that something's going on. But I can't put my finger on it."

"Commander Looker and I will be aboard the Roosevelt in the morning. I'll stay on top of it for you. You know what you can do."

"Yes, Padre. I'll talk with the Lord about it and for your safe flight."

"Thanks, Jake." He grabbed a file from RP1 and was out the door.

"He's in a hurry," RP1 said. "He doesn't want to miss the COD flight."

"I should be on my way too. I need to get home for supper. See you Sunday."

Chapter Thirty

Sandy came into camp with a couple of fish she'd speared for supper.

"Hi, Dad. Will the radio be charged enough to try the 'Mayday' signal before supper?"

"It's as good as it's going to get. I think our best shot will be to turn it on just before sunset. At that time of day, we'll get the most range we can. If a ship or plane comes within twenty to twenty-five miles of us, they should be able to pick it up."

"I'll prep the fish and get the fire started. Then I'll get some fresh fruit. I'll even make some of that coconut glaze you like for the fish."

"Sounds great. I'll go to the pond and wash up and bring some fresh water back to fill the reservoir. If we time this right, we can have what sounds like a great supper, and then flip the switch on the radio. I know it doesn't seem like the signal's getting picked up by anyone. But if we don't try, it won't be picked up for sure."

"I trust the Lord," Sandy said. "He watches over us all the time and takes good care of us. Maybe today's signal will be heard. If not, whenever the battery's recharged, we'll send it again."

"I admire your optimism. You're growing into a strong young woman. You can do anything you set your mind to."

"Thanks, Dad. I love you."

David left camp for the pond. Sandy started the fire and prepped the fish. She went to the grove and picked a mango, a papaya and a coconut. Back at camp she mixed a glaze of fruit juice and coconut, applying it liberally to the fish as she placed them over the fire on three-foot long sticks.

"Something smells really good," David said, returning to camp. "I could eat roasted fish the way you fix it every day. Oh, I guess I do."

"Ha, ha," Sandy laughed. "You can steam clams for supper tomorrow."

"I'll be happy to. Looks like the fish are about ready. Let's thank the Lord and enjoy."

While they ate, Sandy and David talked about their time on the island and the short time Jake had been with them.

"After that scrumptious meal the Lord blessed us with," Sandy said, "I'm feeling hopeful that our signal will be heard. I'll pray for God's blessing and you can flip the switch."

———— • ● • ————

The Legacy's cruise, with all female trainees under Mac's watchful eye, took them on a westerly course toward New Zealand, the halfway point of the cruise. Mac insured the evening watch party finished chow and relieved their counterparts. He heard trainee Lorrie, on radio watch for the evening, yell for him. "I heard a

'Mayday' signal Mac. I heard a 'Mayday' signal."

The First Mate stuck his head in the hatch. "What?" Mac said gruffly.

"I picked up a 'Mayday' on the radio," Lorrie said. "What should I do?"

"Try and reply."

"This is the Legacy responding to your Mayday," Lorrie said. "What is your situation? Over."

Garbled with static the reply came back, "…two… shipwrecked… an island…"

"I'll tell the Captain," Mac shouted, ascending the ladder topside.

"Sir, we've picked up a distress call on the VHF radio," Mac said to Captain Clark. "I suggest we get on our boat's radar and comm devices to see if there's anyone else in the area we can triangulate a position with."

Captain Clark laid a map on the table. "Here's our position," he said, drawing a twenty-five-mile radius around it. "The signal's coming from the area in this circle."

"Hey," Mac said. "That area looks close to where we lost and found Jake earlier this summer."

"Certainly is close," Captain Clark said. "The signal could be from the Taylors that Jake mentioned. Let's see if any other ships are around. I'll contact the Australian and American Naval authorities for help as well. Meanwhile, keep our comm tuned in for more distress calls. Let's see if we can pick up a stronger signal to give us a heading and start closing in on it."

"Aye, aye, Sir."

———•●•———

"Did you hear that, Daddy," Sandy cried out. "Somebody heard the 'Mayday.'"

"Yeah, I heard it," David said, sharing her excitement. "Let's wait a bit and send again. Whoever heard us will try to get a bearing on us. We'll keep giving short bursts until the battery dies."

"Daddy, the Lord's bringing someone here to rescue us." She wiped the tears off her cheeks.

"It's time to signal again," David said. "How about you give the message this time."

Sandy picked up the handheld radio and said, "Mayday, mayday. If anyone can hear this please respond. Mayday, mayday. Over."

"This is the Legacy responding to your distress call. What's your situation? Over."

Sandy looked at her dad. "It's Jake's sailboat, the Legacy," she said.

Smiling at her David said, "Talk to them."

"Legacy. Legacy. Come in Legacy. Over."

"This is the Legacy. I've got you strong and clear. My name is Lorrie. What's your situation? Over."

"Lorrie. My name is Sandy Taylor. My father and I are shipwrecked on an island. We're both in good health. We're not sure where we are but we are on the northern end of an island. The sun will be setting soon so we'll light a signal fire. Also, there's not a lot of battery power left for this radio. Over."

"Copy that, Sandy. Save your radio for one more transmission in an hour. We'll use it for another bearing and watch for your fire. Legacy out."

Mac and Captain Clark stood outside the hatch listening to the radio conversation.

"You did a good job," Mac said to Lorrie. "We've narrowed down the search area to one quarter of the pie. Another bearing in an hour should put us on a line right for the Taylors."

"I'm in touch on my SAT phone through the Roosevelt with the pilot of a COD flight on its way to the USS Roosevelt from USS Enterprise," Captain Clark said. "I'll pass on our course and give them our final bearing in an hour. It'll be dark by then. They can match our position and bearing and do a fly over and with a little luck pick up the signal fire."

Sandy and her dad gathered wood to stack on the beach for a signal fire.

"We need to get enough wood to keep this fire going all night," David said. "You go ahead and start a small fire on the open beach up from where the tide line is. We don't want the tide to come in and put the fire out. I'll continue to gather wood. Some bigger pieces from the tree line I can drag here. When we've got a good core fire going, we'll lay them on top. They'll take longer to burn."

"I'll get it started Dad, but first let's thank the Lord."

"Honey, I've been thanking Him all along."

"I know Dad. Me too. Let's thank Him together."

"Father, in Your goodness you've provided for all of our needs while we've been on this island," Sandy prayed. "You even sent Jake here to give us access to the radio that today connected us with rescuers. Keep those who are coming to our rescue safe. Lead them here by the light of this fire. For Jesus' sake."

"And Lord," David added. "Thanks for keeping my Sandy safe and bringing her back to me. Amen."

Sandy started the fire. David dragged larger pieces of wood to a pile for later. He hugged his daughter and they sat down to wait.

———•●•———

LT Doug Ames, pilot of the COD enroute to the USS Roosevelt from the USS Enterprise made the course adjustment asked for by Captain Clark.

"Commander Looker and Chaplain Evans," LT Ames called to the two passengers on the intercom. "We've been diverted to help with a rescue operation. We're providing overwatch to pick up a signal fire. The sailboat Legacy caught a 'Mayday' call and is on a course toward it. I've diverted a little south of our original flight plan to provide overwatch. We should intersect the Legacy in roughly two hours. We'll take our bearing from her and see what we can see."

"Do you know any details about those needing the rescue?" Commander Looker asked.

"Sounds like two individuals are shipwrecked on an uncharted island. We're supposed to watch for a signal fire. In the dark we should see a fire for miles. When we do, we'll take a position and relay it to Roosevelt and Legacy."

LT Ames heard Commander Looker over the intercom. "Well, Padre, what do you think? The Taylors?"

"I don't see you smile like that very often, John," Chaplain Evans responded. "I know what you always say. 'Some things are meant to be smiled at.' This would sure be one of them."

"LT Ames, after we align with the Legacy, Padre and I can help watch for the signal fire," Commander Looker said. "I'll take the port side Padre, and you take the starboard."

"God bless this rescue effort," Padre said.

"Amen to that," LT Ames replied.

Chapter Thirty-one

Jake and his mom shared the day's events with each other as they ate the meal she had readied that morning. While Jake ate breakfast, he watched her fix a pork loin and put it into the slow cooker. She added carrots and potatoes to the mix as well.

"That was great, Mom. I love what you can do with the slow cooker. You're the best."

"Thanks, honey. I made key lime pie for dessert."

"I'm full, Mom. Supper filled me up. I'll have my pie later after my homework," Jake said, leaving the table.

Jake walked into his room and stretched out on his bed. *Man am I tired. I think a little nap is in order and then I'll hit the books.* In a matter of minutes, he fell asleep.

"Hi Mic," Jake said realizing he was in a subconscious state looking down on himself asleep once again. "How do you decide when I'll see you? It doesn't seem to be random."

"You see us when you have need," Mic said. "Your life intersects with many others providing opportunities for you. The Lord's plan unfolds for you and for others. Don't let Luce's lies lead you away from the path you choose."

"What lies are you talking about?" Jake asked.

"Awareness that lies will come empowers resistance," Cal said. "You are aware. Remember."

"Right," Jake said with a tone of exasperation. "Where's Ace tonight?"

"Ace, Cal and I worked the wind and currents to bring the Legacy close enough to pick up the Taylor's 'mayday' call. Cal insured the sunlight would charge the VHF radio's battery. He used the three of us to create an opportunity for rescue. The COD flight enroute to the USS Roosevelt plays the final piece of the plan. Ace tends the Taylor's rescue fire so that it will burn bright.

"With luck they'll pick up the fire," Jake said.

Mic smiled at Jake. "It won't be luck, but the Lord. For now, you rest and remember."

Jake woke up from his nap trying to figure out what Mic and Cal were talking about. *I'm sure it'll make sense at some point.* He went to his desk and opened his math book but his mind focused on something else, someone else, Sandy. *Why is it whenever I see angels, I think of Sandy?*

"Lord, whatever's going on with Sandy and her dad please keep them safe," Jake prayed. "Mic talked about lies and fire and opportunities. Help me understand what that means, Lord. I ask this in Jesus' powerful name. Amen."

— • ● • —

"An hour has past," David said. "I think we should signal the Legacy again. It'll most likely drain the battery, so it'll take days to recharge, but I think it's our best opportunity for rescue."

Sandy led the way from the signal fire back to camp. David put his arm around her as she flipped the switch on. "Legacy. Legacy. Come in Legacy. This is Sandy. Over."

"Hello, Sandy. This is Lorrie. I read you loud and clear. Have you lit a signal fire? Over."

"Yes, we lit the fire. We'll keep it burning all night. Over."

"Sandy, we've got a line on your signal and are sailing your way," Lorrie said. "Be advised a COD flight on its way to the USS Roosevelt will be flying overwatch out in front of the Legacy on our heading looking for your fire. Once spotted, they'll map your exact position for us. You should hear them when they fly over. It may take… days until we arrive… find you. Over."

"Lorrie, your last sentence broke up. Did you say it would take days for you to find us? Over."

"The battery's dead," David said. "Let's go back to the beach and keep the fire burning bright. Even miles away, a plane flying over will see it. As Lorrie said we should be able to hear it too. I'm encouraged that our rescue's going to happen."

"Me too, Dad. I just wish I knew what that last sentence really said."

"I know. But we need the plane to get our position. No matter what, with that information we'll get rescued sooner or later. Like you said earlier today, the Lord's provided everything we need to survive. So, no worries."

———— • ● • ————

"Commander Looker, Chaplain Evans," LT Ames said into the intercom. "We're flying over the Legacy. If you look out the window, you'll see her running lights below."

"There she is," Commander Looker replied.

After a beat LT Ames said, "Now we watch the horizon for the signal fire."

"I'll watch out the port side," Commander Looker said.

"I've got the starboard side," Chaplain Evans said. "First one to spot the fire gets a special blessing from the Lord."

Ten minutes later LT Ames heard the announcement.

"There it is," the copilot, LTJG (Lieutenant Junior Grade) Randy Davis, and Chaplain Evans said at the same time.

"At 2 o'clock on the horizon," LTJG Davis said.

LT Ames banked slightly to the right and aimed the nose of the COD right at the flickering light in a slow descent. A few minutes before they passed over the fire he turned on the landing lights and saw the two survivors waving at them. He could see the smiles on their faces. He tipped the wings up and down, turned the lights off and took a heading toward the Roosevelt.

"Did you get the GPS location of the fire?" Lt Ames asked LTJG Davis.

"Roger that, Sir. I've already sent it to the Legacy and the Roosevelt. I think we made their day."

"This one feels good, Randy," LT Ames said.

"Let's enjoy it for a moment."

"Hey LT," Chaplain Evans said. "You know that special blessing from the Lord that I mentioned. All of us feel it."

"Copy that, Padre," Commander Looker said.

———•●•———

"They saw us," Sandy said, tearing up. She looked at her dad and saw the tears in his eyes and cried even more.

"God be praised," David said. "They know where we are. Tonight, we praise the Lord and rest. Tomorrow, we start preparing for our departure."

Chapter Thirty-two

A quiet week of preparation changed dramatically when Jake and Stubby left school after Thursday football practice. As Jake turned to drive into the housing area, a crowd of reporters swarmed the truck. *They must have been watching for me.*

Jake and Stubby sat there stunned by all the attention.

"What do they all want?" Stubby asked.

Jake rolled down his window. "What's up?"

A slew of questions came at him. "Was he the boy that spent ten days overboard? Had he heard survivors were found? What did he know? Was he alone on an island with a girl? How come he was rescued and they weren't? What's he hiding?"

"Enough of this stuff," Stubby said. "Roll up your window, honk your horn and let's drive through them and get home."

"That got ugly fast," Jake said. "What's wrong with reporters?"

Once they got through the reporters and into the housing area it hit Jake like a ton of bricks. *They said survivors were found.*

He hit the brakes and pulled to the curb. "You

don't suppose they found Sandy and her dad?"

"Maybe so, but don't get your hopes up. Let's wait for some official word. We can check with Padre's RP at the base chapel and ask him if he's heard anything."

Jake pulled out his cell and made the call and put it on speaker. "RP1 Owens, have you heard anything from Chaplain Evans since he left?"

"It's been radio silence since he left. If I hear anything I promise to let you know."

"Thanks, RP1."

"Where did the reporters get their information from?" Stubby asked. "We need to find an inside source."

"You're right. And I know just who to ask, Jimmy Smith, the school reporter. I bet he knows how to find out. I could promise him an exclusive story if he'll help us."

"That sounds like a plan, Bro."

Jake pulled up Jimmy's number and made the call, putting his phone on speaker again.

"Hey, Jimmy. This is Jake Huber. How ya doin?"

"I'm great. What's up Jake?"

"You remember I was going to give you a story about Stubby's and my overboard experience from early in the summer?"

"Sure, I do. You want to set a time to meet?"

"Yes, but there's more to it now. Stubby and I just got swarmed by a pack of reporters asking all kinds of questions about it. They also asked if we'd heard survivors had been found. Can you find out what the reporters know and how they found out? If you can help us find out where they're getting their information from, I'll give you my story exclusively."

"Wow. It's a deal. I'll be in touch."

"Short of hearing from Padre, Jimmy will get us the information," Jake said.

"Great," Stubby said. "Now, take me home. I need food. You can call me if you hear from anyone."

"I can do that," Jake said, putting his truck in gear.

Chapter Thirty-three

Sandy walked to the beach for her Thursday morning swim and looked out to sea. There a few hundred yards from shore sat a four masted sailboat dropping anchor.

"Dad," Sandy yelled. "A sailboat. It could be the Legacy."

David came through the trees. "Don't just stand there," he said, smiling at her. "Swim out to them and let them know we need rescue."

Sandy ran headlong into the surf and swam to the boat. As she approached, a big Aussie threw a life preserver and line to her.

"Grab ahold," he yelled. "We'll put a ladder over the side for you."

Sandy climbed up the ladder and onto the deck with the help of two crew members.

"Hi. I'm Lorrie. We talked on the radio. This is our first mate, Mac."

"I'm Sandy Taylor. That's my dad on shore. We are so happy you've found us."

"Glad to have you aboard," Mac said. "Your dad a swimmer or should we send a dingy for him?"

"Send the dingy. We have a few personal things

we'll want to bring. I'll swim back in and help my dad gather them. By the time the dingy gets to shore we'll be ready to go. By the way, where are you heading?"

"Auckland, New Zealand's our next port of call," Mac said. "We'll be happy to take you there with us."

"Oh, I have one more question," Sandy said. "Is this the Legacy that Jake Huber crewed on?"

"One and the same," Mac said. "He went overboard and ten days later a Seahawk from the USS Roosevelt rescued him way west of here. A few days later they deposited him right back on this deck."

"Wait. Jake's alive? You found him?"

"Aye, Missy," Mac said. "He had us looking for you and your island for a few days. We never looked this far from where we found him though."

"Where is he now?" Sandy asked.

"He and his crew of trainees finished their training and went ashore on Oahu a few weeks ago," Mac said. "They got off and a new set of trainees came aboard."

"I'm one of the new trainees," Lorrie said. "There's fifteen of us, all girls."

"We have one empty berth that you and your father can stay in," Mac said. "Once we get the two of you settled, we'll weigh anchor and be off to Auckland. The wind is favorable so we should be there inside of a week."

"I'll swim in and get my dad and things ready for the dingy to bring us aboard," Sandy said. "I don't know how I can thank you enough. The Legacy's overboard survivor bag provided the VHF radio for us to signal with. We've already repacked it. We'll bring it with us and it'll have come full circle. It's a God thing."

Sandy dove over the side and swam back to shore.

She and her father secured the camp for future occupants. They each grabbed a bag and the survival bag and waited on the beach for the dingy and their future.

Chapter Thirty-four

His cell phone ringing, pulled Jake away from prepping for a math quiz.

"Hey, Jimmy. What'd you find out?"

"Hey, Jake. My sources told me that they found out about survivors on an island through emails from crew members of the Roosevelt. Bits and pieces of information combined with a whole lot of speculation by reporters trying to put together your story from weeks ago and this new stuff caused quite a stir. You telling your story will get it straightened out."

"I'll be happy to share it with you once I find out for sure about the survivors."

"As far as I can tell a COD on its way to the Roosevelt helped the Legacy with the rescue. If you have any connections with either of them, I'd suggest you try and make contact."

"Thanks. I will."

Jake's email notification signal chirped. He read the message from Chaplain Evans.

"Jake. The Taylors have been found. Rescued today by the Legacy. Will arrive in Auckland within the week. Long story for another time. Chaplain Evans."

"Mom, they've been rescued" Jake yelled at the

top of his lungs.

He ran to the living room where she was reading.

"They've been rescued," Jake said. "I just got an email from Chaplain Evans. There wasn't a lot of info but Sandy and her dad are on the Legacy of all things. They'll be in Auckland within a week. It's amazing. It's a God thing, right?"

"Honey, that's wonderful and yes, it's a God thing."

"Thank You, God," Jake said. "I've gotta tell Stubby and the girls."

"Be careful. Be careful what information you give out and who you give it to."

"I will, Mom. Stubby and the girls I trust. I'll only share the news with them for now."

Jake went out on the lanai and sat down. He sent a group text to Stubby, Carson, Jan, Sue, and Mae. He told them what he knew for sure about the rescue and that he would see them tomorrow at school.

His phone rang. It was Stubby.

"Hey, Stubby. I was just going to call you."

"You gotta be faster than that. So, give me the inside scoop."

"I got an email from Chaplain Evans. There wasn't a lot of information. The text I sent had what Padre's email said. The Taylors are on the Legacy and will be in Auckland within a week."

"Man, that is too cool. You need to get to Auckland next week."

"How am I gonna do that?"

"I don't know. Let's figure something out. In your now famous words, let's pray about it."

"Okay, you're right. See you in the morning."

Jake hung up and starred up at the full moon and starry sky. *Sandy's looking at that same moon and stars. I wonder what she's thinking.*

Chapter Thirty-five

The Legacy sailed in the South Pacific east of New Zealand. Sandy stood next to her dad on deck with Captain Clark taking in the brilliance of the nighttime sky.

"It never gets old does it, Dad," Sandy said.

"When there are no city lights around, the beauty of God's creation stands out," he said.

"Such a beautiful night," Captain Clark said. "With the sails full and no engine noise, the quiet adds to the beauty."

"I talked with God every day about being rescued," Sandy said. "Now that we have, I'm kind of at a loss. I gave God a big thank you. But then what?"

"That's a normal reaction after you've been cut off from the world for so long," Captain Clark said. "Give yourself a little time and everything will fall into place."

"Remember," David said. "It's God's plan that's playing out in you and through you. Keep Him in your heart and whatever the future holds you will be blessed."

"Daddy, I need to figure out how to connect back up with Jake. I feel like the Lord brought us together in this crazy way and I need to see him again."

"Jake told me all about you two," Captain Clark said. "As I recall, he said he shared a special connection with you, too. It was strong enough that he kept insisting the Australian and American forces afloat continue searching for you. I'm still amazed we couldn't locate the island. It was like looking for a needle in a haystack. Only we didn't know the location of the haystack either."

"It was all in God's timing," David said. "We'll see what He has in store for us tomorrow. Sandy let's, you and I, call it a day. Good night, Captain."

Captain Clark shared a good night with the Taylors and they went below to their berth. Sandy continued to have thankfulness on her mind.

Chapter Thirty-six

The Friday before the first football game of the season found Jake contemplating the big day. He remembered that class time would be shortened so the students could participate in a pep rally after the last bell. He and his teammates would be wearing their game jerseys all day. After the rally his team would have a light practice to stretch and loosen up. They would go over final details for the game, and then the boys would be free until Saturday's pregame locker room meeting.

Stubby picked up Jake and they were off to school. Both wore their white home game football jersey trimmed in the blue and orange school colors.

"Do you know what today is?" Stubby asked.

"Yeah. It's Friday. What about it?"

"Hey man. Today is the first day of the rest of your life. It's a day about football and a rescued girl. Both have had big impacts on you. Both will be on your mind. But tomorrow we have the singular purpose to be focused on the game and play our best. So, let's try and deal with your Sandy's rescue today. That leaves tomorrow for football."

"What are you, my therapist now?" Jake asked

sarcastically. "I know I have to keep my head in the game. Come on man, you're preaching to the choir."

"I'm your best friend and I always have your back. This girl is responsible for rewiring your brain. I mean that in a good way. I know you want to do the best you can for her. And I know you want to do the best for the team. Just keep your focus in the right place at the right time."

"I hear you, Stubby. I don't think those two are mutually exclusive. Having Sandy and football on my mind falls under an umbrella of doing my best in all things for Jesus. No matter what I do, He's number one and everything else is subject to Him. Does that make sense?"

"Maybe. You're telling me that anything you do will be done under His guidance and direction."

"Yeah. That's what I'm telling you."

"Okay. Moving on. How do you want to handle the horde of reporters that'll be waiting for you at school?"

"Actually, they will be waiting for both of us. Remember, you were part of the overboard adventure with me."

"Yeah. But I'm just a minor player in the scheme of things. You know they're gonna want to ask you questions."

"When we get to school, we're going to smile and walk right through them. I'm the starting fullback, remember. Just follow me. I'll make a hole to the door."

"I guess your mind is on the game." Stubby grinned. "What you don't know, is that I talked with our teammates and the entire team will be outside the door waiting for us to arrive."

Pulling into the parking lot, Jake saw reporters everywhere. Then he saw the entire football team lined up with many fellow students behind them.

"So cool," Jake said, seeing the team in a gauntlet from the curb to the door.

"Our brothers looking out for us," Stubby said. "I'm going to pull up to the curb and we'll get out and walk up in that line right to the door. Pretty much the whole school's got our backs."

"Man, I don't know what to say."

The scene with his teammates and classmates humbled Jake. He and Stubby got out of the car and were immediately surrounded by students and ushered into the line of players. Jake saw Jan jump into Stubby's car and pull away. Then he heard it in his mind. *Remember*. That's when he knew he wanted everyone of those kids to be with him on the new earth with Jesus.

Jake and Stubby gave high fives to every player down the line. Mr. Phillips, their chem teacher, opened the door to let them in. They were followed by teammates and students and noise until the entry way and hallways were jammed.

"How do you like the pre-pep rally?" Stubby asked.

"I love you, man," was all Jake could say as he gave Stubby a fist bump.

"Hey, sailor," Carson said with a smile. "Is this cool, or what?"

Jake looked up at her and before he could answer, Mae and Sue were there adding their hellos.

"We should start every day like this," Sue said patting Jake and Stubby on their backs.

Then the bell rang. Jake and his friends went to their first hour class, leaving a state of normalcy to reign in the hallway once again. Jake figured the crowd of reporters left outside would write their versions of what they had just seen.

He spent a minute in his first hour class updating the girls about Chaplain Evans' email.

"I wish I could figure out a way to get to Auckland next week," Jake said. "But I'd need to take off school and football practice, not to mention the cost. What a bummer."

"Hey, man," Stubby said. "Keep your mind on the main thing. Sandy and her dad were rescued. They're on their way home. You not being there won't change a thing."

"Wait," Sue said with a questioning look at Jake. "This girl you spent time on an island with is an Aussie named Sandy?"

"Yeah, Sandy Taylor," Jake said.

"She's the one who told you about Jesus and faith that you mentioned to me a while back?"

"Yeah, that's her."

"I know her," Sue said. "We met when my dad worked in Australia for a time and I went along with him. I enjoyed surfing during his meetings. One day, surfing off a port town beach, I met Sandy swimming. We ended up seeing a lot of each other until she and her dad left for fishing. That was about fifteen months ago."

"Amazing," was the only word Stubby could come up with.

"That is way beyond coincidence," Carson said.

Jake didn't have words. He was speechless. *Lord,*

help me figure a way to get to Auckland and see Sandy.

The bell rang and math class began. For the remainder of the day classes whizzed by for Jake due to the shortened class time schedule. The final bell rang and everyone made their way out to the football field for the pep rally. Jake and Stubby sat with the team. The students filled the bleachers. The cheerleaders and band took the field, taking turns getting everyone fired up. The coach introduced each team member to thunderous applause. The band played the school's fight song. When it ended, Saturday's game was tee'd up. They were ready.

"Stubby," Jake said. "This school day is ending on a high note just like it began. I think I'm in a daze."

"Yep. You've been in a cloud all day especially when you found out Sue knew Sandy. I'm still trying to wrap my brain around that."

"I feel like ever since I went overboard, God's been putting Sandy in the middle of my life. I know it doesn't matter if I'm there or not when the Legacy gets in. But something inside of me makes me feel like I should be. I just don't know."

"I hear ya, man. But here's the deal. They don't get in till the end of the week. Our first game is tomorrow. You need to make that a priority and get your head in the game now."

"Okay, okay, you're right. But I need to do one thing first."

Jake pulled out his cell and dialed up Jimmy Smith.

"Hey, Jimmy. It's Jake. Stubby and I are by the goal post. How about meeting us with your pen and pad?"

"I'll be there in a minute."

"We're going to give him the whole overboard story in summary version," Jake said to Stubby. "Then, when we run into any reporters, we can point them in his direction. I know they won't like it, but it'll help keep the narrative straight."

"That's actually a pretty good idea," Stubby said.

"Hey, guys," Jimmy said, walking up to them. "I've got my pad. I also have a small voice recorder. Do you mind?"

"Not at all," Jake said.

Jake explained his plan to Jimmy who said he would be happy to accommodate. As Stubby and Jake began sharing their story, Carson, Jan, Sue and Mae stopped by. Soon several teammates gathered around to listen in.

"I found out by email from Chaplain Evans yesterday," Jake said winding the story up, "that the crew of the Legacy had rescued the Taylors. That's the sailboat that Stubby and I trained on when we went overboard in the first place."

"So, now you know the truth of it," Stubby said. "If you hear anything different, feel free to speak to it."

"I saw some things online this afternoon that weren't very flattering of you Jake," Jan said. "I think reporters make stuff up as they go along."

"I can't wait to see the next edition of some of the tabloids," Mae said.

"Well, Jimmy's got the real story," Jake said. "Once he gets it out there, some people will look pretty foolish."

"Jimmy, how about walking to my car with us," Stubby said. "Just in case any reporters are lurking in the parking lot."

"Sure thing," Jimmy said. "Once I get your story written, I'll email a copy to you both before I submit it. If you have any concerns let me know."

"Thanks, Jimmy," Jake said. "Let's go."

As the three boys approached Stubby's car, a lone reporter stood waiting. She worked for the local paper.

"Talk to Jimmy," Stubby said. "He's our publicist."

Stubby and Jake got into Stubby's car and left the reporter in the capable hands of Jimmy.

"Easy peesy plan to avoid the press," Stubby said. "Now, let's get your mind solely on a football game that's happening tomorrow."

"Copy that," Jake said.

Chapter Thirty-seven

Jake entered the locker room and found it abuzz with a low frequency hum of soft conversation and thought. Players get ready for games in different ways. Some are quiet. Some are loud. Some nap. Some stare. Others keep their mind's eye on the challenge in front of them.

Players stood in line to get their ankles taped. Players in various stages of dress put uniform pads in place.

Jake sat down in front of his locker. *It's game day Lord. Please help me to play hard and give my best effort.*

"Hey, Jake," Stubby said, slapping him on the back bringing him back to reality. "You ready for this?"

"I am so ready. All the stupid press that came out this morning has me really fired up. What Jimmy wrote is gonna help. I'll be glad when his article hits the street. In the meantime, I'm pretending that every guy I hit on the field is a reporter."

"Sounds like a plan," Stubby said. "Let's go tear them up."

Jake's team won the coin toss and scored on their first possession. Stubby caught a quick pass in the flat and Jake provided a key block to let him in the endzone. After that it became a defensive game until the other team scored early in the third quarter. Some of the players on the rival team were making it a point to trash talk at Jake. He figured they had seen some of the false reporting about him on the internet.

Lord, Mic said there would be lies. So please don't let this junk bother me. Help me use it to my advantage.

The game was tied 7 to 7 with two minutes to go in the fourth quarter. On the third down of their possession, Jake made a fake run up the middle, the quarterback kept the ball and rolled out into the flat and threw across the field to a wide-open Jake who caught the pass and ran fifteen yards for the touchdown. The crowd went wild. Jake's team ended up winning 14 to 7.

"That's what I'm talking about," Jake yelled to no one in particular.

After the post-game team huddle on the field, Jake headed to the locker room with his team. Showered and dressed and ready to celebrate, Jake and Stubby walked to the parking lot.

"Jan's invited a small group of us to her house," Stubby said. Her dad put an eleven pm curfew on it. Wanna go?"

"Sure. How about we swing by my house and drop off my truck. I'll jump in with you and we can go together."

"Great. I'll follow you to your house. On the way, I'll let my mom know what I'm doing."

"Okay, see you at my house."

The drive from school to the housing area and Jake's took less than fifteen minutes. Jake jumped in with Stubby and they were off to Jan's.

"It's pretty cool that Jan's parents are letting her have this party," Stubby said.

"Yea, but you know why. If they host, they can keep a watchful eye on things. And unlike a lot of parents, they will."

"So true," Stubby said with his usual grin. "Look, there's still a spot in Jan's driveway and my car will fit right in."

Jake and Stubby were greeted at the front door with a sign that said, "Please go around back." They followed the walkway around the side of the garage. In the back they found Jan and Carson and several of their friends. GySgt. McBride stood at the grill cooking hot dogs and hamburgers. Mrs. McBride worked in the kitchen getting side dishes ready to bring out.

"Here they are," Jan said. "The heroes of the day."

When the clapping died down Jake said, "You all are as much heroes as we are. You're the best fans in the world. Your loud cheering kept the other team back on their heels as much as our playing did."

"But you two scored the touchdowns that gave us the win," Carson said. "Let's celebrate!"

"I have one request," Jake said. "Tomorrow morning I'd like all of you to go to church and give thanks to God. If you don't have a church, the base chapel has plenty of room. See ya there."

Silence. Stubby came to Jake's rescue. "Jake's not throwing a wet blanket on this party. He wants to add to the celebration by continuing it in church tomorrow."

"On that note, the food's ready," GySgt. McBride said. "Come and get it."

The food brought the celebration back to life and

Jake thought everyone seemed to be having a good time.

"Hey, bro," Stubby said. "That invitation might have been just a little over the top timing wise."

"I know. Something inside told me I should just put it out there."

"Yeah, I get it. But maybe more of a one-on-one approach would be better. Work the ground a little before you throw the seed out there."

"You could be right. But thanks for having my back."

"I do. Now, let's eat."

"One more thing," Jake said. "You were very philosophical just now."

"Thanks. Now can we eat?"

The kids ate their fill of the McBride party feast and celebrated the high points, and some low points, of the game. Eleven o'clock came quickly. Gunny announced the party's end.

"Drive home safely, everyone," Jan said. "I'm glad you could all be here tonight to celebrate the victory."

"Thanks for having us." Carson hugged her good-bye.

"Ditto that," Jake said. "Thanks for supporting the team. See you all in school Monday."

"I, for one, will see you tomorrow in church," Stubby said with his ever-present grin.

A couple of the kids said, "Me too," in the background.

Jake felt a shiver go up his spine. *I bet Mic, Ace and Cal smiled hearing all that.*

He went inside and thanked Gunny and Mrs. McBride for hosting the party.

"I like the way you're influencing your friends in such positive ways," Gunny said. "See you tomorrow."

It was a quick drive to Jake's. He opened his door.

"Want me to pick you up in the morning? My mom's working the weekend shift, so it'll just be you and me."

"Sure thing. See you in the AM."

He closed the door and went in the house, told his mom good night and went to his room. Just as he sat down his cell rang. Sue's name popped up.

"Hey, Sue. What's happening?"

"Hi, Jake. I thought if that offer to go to church with you still stands, I'd like to go."

"It absolutely does. Stubby's riding with me so I'll pick you up about 9:15. That'll get us to the base chapel in plenty of time for the service. My mom's working this weekend, so it'll just be the three of us."

"Okay, I'll be ready. My dad's been out of town and not due back till tomorrow night. I thought it might be a nice time to check out the base chapel."

"That's great."

"Besides, when I figured out that the Sandy I knew from Australia was the same Sandy of your uncharted island, I needed to connect up with you. She's a special person and if you're connected to her from a spiritual perspective, then I want to connect with you too."

"Sounds like she had an impact on you too."

"She did in an amazing way. She's not your run of the mill Christian. She's a follower of Jesus real-time."

"Yeah, I know what ya mean. Well, it's late so I'm going to hit the rack. See ya in the morning."

"Good night, Jake. See you then."

———•●•———

The Sunday morning worship evoked less enthusiasm than the previous week. Chaplain Evans deployed on the Roosevelt, left the service in the hands of another Protestant Chaplain, Jack Ecker, who led the service and preached. As Sundays go, Jake didn't think it anything spectacular. *No matter who's leading worship, God is still here with us. We praise. We pray. We give thanks to God for His blessing in our lives, and we remember.*

During fellowship time following worship, Jake sat with Stubby and Sue at a table with Carson and Jan and two of their friends from the party. The white powdered sugar remains of a jelly donut encircled Stubby's mouth as he chugged a cup of grape juice. Jake enjoyed the lively conversation about the day's message. He thought it special that four of them came because of his invitation. *More is better.* They also talked about the news of the day. Jimmy Smith's article hit the local papers. Then a bombshell landed in Jake's lap.

"Jake, I know you feel a strong connection to Sandy Taylor," Sue said. "I do too. It just so happens that my dad has a business trip to Melbourne, Australia on Wednesday. I told him about Sandy's rescue and that the Legacy would be stopping in Auckland. He's flying on his corporate jet and said he could make a stop in Auckland if I wanted to go with him so that I could see her. I told him about your experience and he said you'd be welcome to come too. What do you think?"

"Are you serious?" Jake asked.

"Absolutely. My dad said he would drop us off in Auckland on Thursday and then pick us up on his way back to Oahu on Saturday. It's a free ride, Jake. How about it?"

"What an amazing opportunity," Stubby said. "Tell her yes, Jake. We have a bye week so no football game to miss on Saturday."

"I'm sure you can get schoolwork from your teachers to work on during the flight," Carson said. "It's a long way."

"This sounds like a God thing," Jake finally said. "I'll talk with my mom this evening but I'm positive she'll say I can go."

"Jake, I have to say, you're one blessed guy," Jan said. "What is it with you and God?"

"Here's what I know," Jake said. "God loves every one of us and wants us to all be with Him on the new earth after the resurrection. That's heaven. Jesus is the way for us to be there. Baptism and faith connect us to Him. It's that simple. Just believe."

"But how do you know?" Derek, one of the friends asked.

"Well, He tells us so in the bible," Jake said. "But I saw Him in heaven 1.0 when I was on the island. It's the real deal. But even so, the guys who wrote the New Testament of the Bible saw Jesus for real. Paul and John even saw heaven 1.0 too. I guess it comes down to how many eyewitness accounts do you need to believe what they say is true."

"That's the most passionate witness I've ever heard," Chaplain Ecker said, walking up to the table. "I'm not sure I've seen you here at the chapel before."

"Today is three weeks in a row and counting,"

Stubby said. "Jake invited the four of us to come here today."

"God be praised, Jake," Chaplain Ecker said. "Let's talk more some time. God bless you all."

Chaplain Ecker moved on to greet folks at another table.

"I don't know about the rest of you," Stubby said, "But I'm ready for some real food. How about it?"

"This would be a great day for a pizza lunch," Carson said. "Any of you interested?"

"The magic number is five," Jake said. "Let's meet at the pizza place just outside the gate."

"I'm with you," Stubby said.

"Me too," Sue and Jan chimed in together.

Chapter Thirty-eight

Jake arrived at the airfield at 2 on Wednesday morning, passport in one hand and backpack over his shoulder. Based on the day's weather, he wore grey shorts and a burgundy polo shirt. He walked up to Sue and her dad. He stood a head taller than her dad, a shorter man of Asian descent. Sue looked a lot like him. Her floral top with yellow pastel pants complimented him. *Great minds think alike. She looks very nice.*

"Hey, Sue, looking good. I'm ready to go."

"Hey, Jake. Let me introduce you to my dad, Chen Yang. Dad, this is Jake."

"Good morning, sir. Thanks so much for letting me come with you and Sue. I can't wait to see Sandy safe and sound."

"From what my daughter tells me, you and Sandy have an even more special thing then she and Sandy have. I'm happy to have empty seats filled on my jet. With all the climate enthusiasts out there, a full plane is a good thing."

"All the same, I really appreciate it."

"Well, let's get through customs and get aboard. Once we're seated, they'll bring us breakfast. After that I hear you and Sue have some schoolwork to do. I'll be in my airborne office on a conference call for most of the morning. So, I'll see you at lunchtime.

"Thanks again for letting me come along."

Sue grabbed Jake by the arm. "This way to customs."

Jake followed Sue and her dad through customs and on to the plane. The cabin of the jet reminded Jake of a luxury suite. Light tan overstuffed leather sofas for seating, a galley kitchenette, a large screen smart TV and a dining area led the way to an executive bathroom. Mr. Yang walked through a door at the rear of the cabin marked office. Jake and Sue sat down in the main cabin. They settled in, buckling their seat belts and got ready for takeoff.

Soon the jet rolled down the runway and lifted off. The flight attendant came by taking breakfast orders.

"I'll have eggs, ham and hashbrowns," Jake said.

"You're in luck. We happen to have that exact meal ready to go. Would you like juice or coffee with it?'

"Do you have V-8?"

"Yes, we do."

"That's what I'd like."

"I'll have the same," Suc said. "With a side of whole wheat toast."

"I'll be right back with it."

The breakfast tasted good to Jake, considering he knew it was made earlier and kept in a warmer till served. Although he wasn't a big coffee drinker Sue talked him into a French vanilla cappuccino.

"The cappuccino isn't half bad," Jake said. "I can see how so many people can make drinking it a habit."

"Wait for the caffeine to kick in," Sue said with a

laugh. "The flight time to Auckland is about eight hours. There's a twenty-two-hour time difference so it'll be one o'clock in the afternoon on Thursday when we arrive. You said the Legacy should be docking around four o'clock so we should have plenty of time to get to the pier before them. My dad's arranged a car for us and lodging for a couple of nights. He also arranged it for the Taylors if they would like it."

"Wow. Your dad's very generous."

"He puts money into things he cares about. He knows how important my relationship with Sandy is to me. You're my new friend and surfing buddy. So, it all works out."

"As busy as it looks like we're going to be, now is probably a good time to get our schoolwork done," Jake said. "That way, after lunch I might take a snooze if I can. I don't want jet lag to slow me down."

"Sounds like an excellent plan. Let's hit the books."

Jake and Sue sat down at the dining table and got to work. Jake worked through math and chem worksheets after reading corresponding chapters in the associated textbook. Lit and history both had assigned readings. Spanish consisted of vocabulary memorization and a worksheet. Jake focused on the work and got it done with time to spare before lunch.

Sue worked with equal efficiency. But instead of Spanish she worked on Chinese. That slowed her down a bit. Eventually she completed her work too.

"I'm glad that's done,' Jake said. "I want to keep my mind focused on the Taylors return to civilization. Actually, Sandy's return. I can't wait to see her."

"I sense there's something more between you and

Sandy than just rescue and Jesus. I mean she shared Jesus with me in a way that was real and personable and I'm so happy about her and her dad's rescue. That much you and I have in common with her. But I think there's more for you."

"Yeah, maybe. We got really close in a friendship kind of way. But I have to say that I feel closer to her than anyone I've ever known. Hopefully, seeing her again will help me understand my feelings better. Know what I mean?"

"No, I don't know what you mean, but I understand. Your friendship sounds like it has some affection with it. That might be something for you to think about. Maybe you already think about it. I think you two are kindred spirits and God brought you together for something special. I can't think of two people better suited to be shipwrecked together than you two."

"Who's being shipwrecked now?" Mr. Yang said, coming out of his office.

"We were just talking about Sandy and Jake on the island," Sue said getting up to give her dad a hug. "I love you, Dad, and your generosity."

"I love you too, my precious. Money and possessions must always take a lessor role to family and friends. I am pleased to help you and Jake welcome your friend home."

Jake's stomach growled. Mr. Yang laughed. "How about we get ready for lunch."

The three took seats at the table. The attendant placed assorted meats, cheeses, and condiments in front of them. Then she passed them a plate with a variety of bread and sandwich rolls. Finally, she passed them a fruit tray.

"What may I serve you to drink," she asked. "I have water, coffee, tea and soda."

Sue and Jake both opted for a bottle of water. Mr. Yang asked for coffee. Then, out of nowhere, Sue asked Jake if he would have a prayer of thanksgiving. She smiled at his surprised look. Jake did the honors.

"Lord, thanks for the food before us, the opportunity for this trip and the safe return of Sandy and her dad. We lay our thanks before you for Jesus' sake. Amen."

"Thank you, Jake," Mr. Yang said. "I am pleased to have met you and look forward to knowing you better."

"Thank you, Mr. Yang. Thanks for all that you're doing for this trip. Especially thanks for inviting me to come along."

"I am happy you were able to come," Mr. Yang said with a smile. "Now let us eat."

"The pilot asked me to share that we should arrive in Auckland within three hours," the attendant said, after clearing the table of the lunch items. "It will be one o'clock on Thursday afternoon."

Jake yawned and stretched out in an easy chair. Sue put some soft tunes on the sound system and laid back too.

"My office responsibilities call me," Mr. Yang said. "I will see you before landing."

"Later, sir," Jake said, closing his eyes.

———• ● •———

Sandy stood on deck at the rail admiring the sunset with her father.

Mac walked up. "We're about five hours from the port at Auckland. Legacy should make port about four o'clock Auckland time. What are yer plans after we dock?"

"I think we'll hail a cab and find a hotel to put us up for a night or two," David said. "We'll have a nice meal, not that the food on this boat wasn't good, a steak and a beer for me. What do you think Sandy?"

"I think a hamburger with all the fixings is what I want, and a plate of French fries with loads of ketchup. Then I'll go back to my normal diet of fruit, salad, and fish."

Mac smiled. "Sounds like you've thought about it for a minute. I like how you both think. I want to share some good news. We'll be tying up to a pier, so you can step right off on to dry land as it were. Captain Clark will let the two of you off first while the crew and trainees rig for port. I suspect there'll be a wad of reporters waiting to talk with you. I wish ya good luck with that."

"Thanks, Mac," David said. "There's a few hours left to enjoy the view and thank the Lord for taking care of us."

"Well, I'll leave ya to it," Mac said turning and walking aft.

"So, we acclimate tonight and then work your plan tomorrow to get in touch with the bank and the insurance company," Sandy said. "Do you have enough cash or credit for tonight since we won't talk to the bank until tomorrow? I mean I know the Lord's taken care of us so far. I'm sure He won't stop now. I'm just thinking out loud."

"Sandy," David said, shaking his head. "We're fine. Captain Clark called ahead and the Legacy office in port will have anything we need for the short term. Once we arrive and get the lay of the land, we'll stop in there. I didn't tell you simply because I just found out from him during lunch while you were taking that navigation lesson from Mac."

"No worries, Dad. After fifteen months away I'm going to have to learn how to be among people again. I'll pray for God's help with that."

———•●•———

"Wheels down in one hour," the pilot said on the intercom. The announcement brought Jake and Sue back to wakefulness. Sue got up and went to the bathroom.

Jake kept hearing in his mind, "Be careful of lies and deceit. Always remember." *That's strange. Hearing voices takes getting used to.* He got up and moved to a window seat. *New Zealand's not that big.* He looked out the window at the ocean below trying to catch a glimpse of the Legacy. The boat would be about fifty or sixty miles out yet. The jet flew too high and too far out to see it.

Sue returned and sat in a window seat on the other side of the cabin. Jake looked over at her.

"We're almost there," she said. "There's a whole lot of ocean down there. Can't see much more than water since we're so high. This is as much fun as waiting to catch a big wave. There's a lot of anticipation and you don't know how it's all going to play out."

Mr. Yang came out of his office.

"We've started our descent for Auckland," he said. "When we arrive, we'll deplane and go through customs. I'll help you connect with your driver. He will have all the information about the hotel I reserved for you, the pier number for the Legacy and so forth. It's all arranged. I'll return to Auckland Saturday afternoon for a six o'clock pm departure for Oahu. That will have us arriving on Oahu Saturday morning around five o'clock am. The driver will have you back here at the airport by four o'clock pm Saturday to go through customs. How does that sound?"

"Sounds great," Jake said.

"Thanks, Dad. If the driver knows all that we can rely on him to remind us. Back here at four on Saturday afternoon, I'll remember."

"Good girl. I have about thirty minutes of work to finish up and then I will rejoin you for the landing."

"See you in a bit," Sue said.

Mr. Yang went back to his office and Sue moved over to sit by Jake.

"You keep staring out the window so intently," Sue said. "What's on your mind?"

"Oh, just trying to see if I can find the Legacy. The lower we descend the more things come into view."

Sue smiled. "You know, Sandy doesn't know we're going to be there at the pier to meet her."

"I know. There'll probably be a few reporters there too. Maybe you should go to greet her and I'll wait in the car. She'll be surprised to see you there. After your hello's you can offer them the car and hotel. Then you can help her and David get through any reporters to the car for surprise number two, me. What do you think?”

“That sounds like a good plan. We can always modify it on the fly as we need to. My dad said that our driver would know all the arrangements about the hotel and the pier Legacy will tie up to. But remember, we’ll need to be back at the airport Saturday afternoon for a 6pm takeoff. So, we’ll have two nights and two days with the Taylors and be back on Oahu Saturday morning.”

“That’s like time travel,” Jake said. “Jet lag will catch up to us by then. I’m pretty sure I’ll be sleeping most of the flight back.”

“Me too. Let me know if you spot the Legacy. I’ll watch out the window on the other side.”

Sue got up and returned to the other side of the cabin. Jake resumed his watch for the Legacy, but his mind went somewhere else, the island with his beautiful companion, the girl of his dreams, Sandy.

No sooner had Mr. Yang come out of his office and taken a seat than Jake spotted the Legacy.

“I see it, the Legacy under full sail headed for Auckland. Such a beautiful sight from up here.”

Sue and her dad both came over to look. As they flew over the Legacy, a sudden updraft made the jet tip its wings back and forth. Jake felt something deep inside himself. *I bet Cal or Ace caused that for Sandy. They always seem ready to assist in our relationship.* Then he heard in his mind. *Remember.*

“She’s really making time with the breeze down there,” Mr. Yang said, bringing Jake back to reality. “She’ll be in port in no time.”

“Please take your seats and buckle your seat belts,” the flight attendant said. “We’ll be landing in a few minutes.”

Jake occasionally thought about pilot skills as they related to being a member of the Space Force. He hadn't considered them from a civilian perspective till now. The jet touched down on the runway. *But for the sound of the tires on concrete we could still be in the air. The pilot's got skills.*

Taxiing up to a private hanger the jet parked by a white limousine. The three travelers climbed down the jet's ladder. Jake and Sue followed Mr. Yang inside for the customs declaration.

“I'll say good-bye for now,” Mr. Yang said. “When you get out front, your driver, Sam, will be waiting for you. As soon as the jet is refueled, I'll be off to Melbourne and my meeting there. I'll meet you here at nine on Saturday evening.”

Sue hugged her dad. “Have a safe trip, Dad. I love you.”

“I love you,” Mr. Yang said. “Please give my greetings to the Taylors. Make sure you enjoy your time with Sandy.”

“Again, thank you Mr. Yang,” Jake said, shaking his hand.

“I'm so excited,” Sue said, grabbing Jake's arm and pulling him along. “Let's go see our friend.”

Chapter Thirty-nine

Sue and Jake walked out to the limo with their bags. Sam had the door and trunk open.

"Welcome to New Zealand," Sam said, placing their bags in the trunk. "I'll provide for your transportation needs and serve as your activity director while you're here in Auckland. If there's anything you need or want, please don't hesitate to ask. I'm at your service."

"How long will it take to get to the harbor and the pier the Legacy will be docking at?" Jake asked.

"About a thirty-minute drive from here. My sources at the harbor said the Legacy should be in port around three-thirty. That's plenty of time if you'd like to stop for a snack or something. I know just the place located right next to a quaint little gift shop. You might see something you'd like to pick up for your friends, the Taylors."

"I could eat something," Jake said. "I'm sure we'll be feasting later this evening with Sandy and her dad. So, maybe a snack would be good to hold me over. What do you think, Sue?"

"I like it. The gift shop is a great idea. I hadn't thought about a memento of the occasion."

"Well Sam, we're in your hands," Jake said.

"Hop in and we'll be off."

It wasn't a full stretch limo, but it could hold six passengers with room to spare. *Not exactly an inconspicuous ride.* Twenty minutes later, Sam pulled to the curb in front of an eatery next to a gift shop. He got out went around to the back door and opened it.

"I'll pick you up here in an hour. Enjoy."

"Thanks, Sam," Sue said, stepping out.

Jake, right behind her half tripped on the curb, but Sam caught him before he hit the deck.

"Thanks, Sam," Jake said. *What a klutz I am.* "How do you trip in tennis shoes?" he said under his breath.

"Slow down till you get your land legs sailor," Sue said, smiling at him. "Let's grab a bite and then we can spend the rest of the time in the gift shop."

Jake suggested they share an appetizer of chips and salsa. Both drank bottled water not wanting local water to cause any possible stomach issues. They had two days and Jake wanted to make the most of them.

Entering the gift shop was like going into a different world for Jake. All sorts of unique gifts lined the shelves. He went one way and Sue went the other. It took twenty-five minutes for Jake to find the perfect remembrance for Sandy. At the register he found Sue waiting with her purchase.

"I have to admit, this was a great idea," Jake said.

"Yes, and we have five minutes to spare. Let's go out to the sidewalk and watch for Sam."

The limo pulled up and Jake opened the door before Sam could get out. Jake said, "No worries," giving Sam a wink.

Ten minutes later the limo parked by the pier. Reporters were hanging around, waiting for the Legacy to come in. Jake could see the masts empty of the sheets. Her diesel motor brought her into the harbor. In no time the Legacy's crew had her tied up to the dock.

Sue got out of the limo and walked to the end of the pier to wait. Jake watched through the darkened limo windows.

"Lord, this is an amazing day," Jake prayed. "Thanks for bringing the Taylors here safely and for getting me here too. You're amazing! Bless this reunion and our time together for Jesus' sake. Amen"

Sue started jumping up and down and Jake caught a glimpse of Sandy walking down the gang plank. Her father followed behind her.

Wow, does she look good. I don't know if I can sit here and wait.

Jake watched Sue and Sandy reunite at the end of the pier in a hug complete with tears of joy. David had his arms around them both.

Jake lowered the window a little so he could hear.

"What are you doing here?" Sandy asked.

"It's a long story and I'll tell you all the details," Sue said. "But first I need to tell you and your dad that my dad arranged for a car and lodging for the two of you for a few days until you get settled into your future. He won't take no for an answer. That white limo over there is our objective as soon as we can clear all the reporters surrounding us."

All three got peppered with questions. Then David raised his hands to calm everyone down. By his size, he intimidated everyone enough that they quieted down.

"I have a statement for you," David said. "My

daughter, Sandy, and I are indebted to the crew of the Legacy and the crew of the USS Roosevelt for our rescue. A tsunami sank my boat near an uncharted island. We spent the past year there. God has taken great care of us and provided for our needs. We give our thanks to Him. We'll have more to say at a later time. Right now, we ask that you give us some space. Thank you."

Jake could hardly contain himself wanting so desperately to hug Sandy. He was like a champagne bottle ready to pop its cork. Then they started moving toward the limo. Sam got out to open the back door. Jake got on the passenger side toward the front so no one would see him when the door opened.

He heard Sue insisting that Sandy get in first. He could tell she held David back. Sandy stepped inside.

"Hey," was all Jake could get out. She put her arms around him like she would never let go. Jake could feel her joyful sobs. He had his arms around her and the two hugged. When the limo door closed it brought them back to reality.

"For the longest time we didn't know if you survived or not," Sandy said, wiping tears from her eyes. "I'm so happy to see you. God be praised." Then she buried her head on Jake's shoulder and sobbed and hugged some more.

"Hi Jake," David said. "I'm glad you're safe and sound. We've talked a lot about you these past weeks. I can't wait to hear the story of your rescue. But first, how on earth did you meet up with Sue?"

"It's a God thing," Jake said. "I've come to realize that my whole life is a God thing, thanks to this girl right here in my arms." He hugged her again.

Epilogue- Chapter Forty

Sam drove the travelers to their hotel. It turned out to be quite a ritzy place near the water in the harbor district. Before exiting the limo, Sue gave Sandy her gift, a pretty blouse and shorts set.

"I knew you wouldn't have much in the clothes department," Sue said. "I thought you could wear this for tonight. Tomorrow we can go shopping for some essentials."

"Thank you," Sandy said. "This is so thoughtful of you."

"I've got something for you too," Jake said handing Sandy a small bag. "When I saw it, I knew I had to get it for you."

Sandy opened the bag and pulled out a small box. She opened it and found a gold chain necklace with a pendant of letters that said "Remember" on it.

"I love it. Help me put it on," she said holding her long blond hair in one hand.

Jake put the necklace around her neck and clasped it for her. She turned and kissed him on the cheek and gave him a hug. Sam opened the door and David stepped out, followed by Sue and Sandy. Jake climbed out last.

"If you need transportation or anything else, please give me a call," Sam said handing his business cards to all four. "Inside you'll find the room reservations in your names. This district has some very nice restaurants within walking distance. But I'm happy to take you anywhere you like."

A hotel attendant put their bags on a cart and led them inside. The hotel looked like a modern version of an older ornate one from the past. Jake thought it must have a five-star rating.

Sue walked up to the front desk, followed by the others. "My father made room reservations for us." She told the desk clerk their names.

"I have three rooms for you," the clerk said. "There is a two-room suite for the Taylors. That would be David and Sandy. Please sign the guest register here."

"Next, I have two single rooms," the clerk went on. "These are for Sue and Jake. Please sign the register as well."

"If you would be so kind as to identify which bags go to your individual rooms for the attendant, he will be happy to deliver them."

Jake grabbed his bag and swung it over his shoulder. Sue grabbed hers and set it on the floor next to her.

"The rest of them go to our room," David said, showing his room number to the attendant. "I propose that we go up to our rooms, which are all on the same floor by the way, get cleaned up a bit and then meet down here in the lobby for supper about seven. Sound good to everyone?"

"I like your plan and I propose an addendum for

it," Jake said. "I'm about as cleaned up as I'm going to get. So, Sandy, if you're ready sooner, come knock on my door. We have lots to talk about. You can grab Sue on your way if you like. No matter what we'll meet down here at seven."

"Good plan," David said. "I'll see you all at seven."

"I'll knock on your door when I've cleaned up a bit," Sandy said.

She grabbed Sue by the arm and the two followed David to the elevator. Jake fell in behind them. *How can I be blessed with two girls like them for friends. Both athletic and good looking and know Jesus. Thank you, Lord.*

An hour later Jake heard a knock on the door. He opened to a refreshed and smiling Sandy who walked in and gave him a hug. He hugged her back. She wore the new outfit that Sue gave her. Jake decided she looked great in whatever she wore.

After a beat Sandy said, "I stopped by Sue's. She didn't want to be a third wheel. So, here I am."

"Happy to see you doesn't even come close to what I'm feeling," Jake said. "You look great. Your hair smells good too. Not that it ever smelled bad." *How could I say such a dumb thing.*

"You can thank Sue for that," Sandy said as she chuckled. "Now let's sit down and you tell me what happened to you."

"Okay. Come on. Let's sit over here on the sofa."

"I want all the details," Sandy said. "When you didn't come back that evening, I didn't know what to think. I turned the worry over to the Lord. I knew He had a plan for you. I didn't know if I was still part of it or not. I thought about you every day since that day you left."

"The Lord continued working His plan," Jake said. "As I swam out north of the island the water got rougher and rougher. I didn't realize that a rip tide pulled me west from the island. A storm came up, tossing me around like a rag doll. I lost sight of the island. Turns out, according to Mic, I ended up where I first went into the water."

Jake related his rescue by the Seahawk to the Roosevelt, his transfer to the Legacy and the search that went on for the island. Not finding it, the Legacy finished her cruise, returning Jake back to MCBH. He shared how he met Sue while surfing, including being hit in the head, another encounter with the three angels, and dolphins getting him to shore safely. He talked about the reporters and their incorrect stories, letting her know there could be more of the same with her.

"All in all, I can look back and see God's hand in everything including your rescue," Jake said. "So, here we are."

"God's at work in all of this. Because of our interaction, the Legacy's survival bag got to dad and me. Yeah, I swam around and got it with the dolphins help. The VHF radio and charger helped us make contact with the Legacy and brought them to us with a little help from the Roosevelt too. So, yes here we are."

Jake put his hand on Sandy's cheek. "I'm glad God had our lives cross paths. I'm glad you're in my life. I pray that it's for a long time."

Someone knocked on the door. Jake opened it to a smiling Sue.

"It's close to seven," she said. "I thought you two

might have lost track of the time. So, I thought I'd come and get you for dinner."

"Why do you have such a big smile on your face?" Jake asked.

"Oh, I saw the connection between you two right away," Sue said. "Let's continue the story telling at the dinner table. I'm thinking Sandy and David might enjoy a meal prepared for them by someone else for a change."

"That does sound good," Sandy said.

"Let's go," Jake said, holding the door for Sandy.

David stood by the elevator waiting. He looked refreshed and at ease.

"Come on, you three," David said. "There's a steak and beer with my name on it in the hotel's restaurant. I checked with the front desk and the clerk said the food here is outstanding. I thought we should check it out for ourselves."

David led the way into the restaurant.

The hostess looked up at him and then at Sandy. "You wouldn't by chance be the Taylors?"

"That's us," David said. "We'd like a table for four."

"Welcome. My name's Diana. We've been expecting you. Please follow me."

Diana escorted them to a beautifully decorated more private area of the restaurant. A great place for conversation, food, and friendship. David shared a word of prayer and then ordered his steak and beer. Sandy had her hamburger with the works and fries with plenty of ketchup. Jake enjoyed seafood fettuccine with a cup of clam chowder. Sue chose salmon and a garden salad.

The four ate and talked and talked some more.

Three hours later, after eating and sharing, they learned that the hotel paid for their meal.

"We are truly blessed," Sandy said. "Right now, I'm tired and ready for a good night's sleep in a real bed."

"Why don't we plan to meet tomorrow morning around nine at our room," David said. "I've got business to attend to and the three of you can make your plans for the day."

They rode up the elevator together and said their goodnights. Sue went down the hall to her room. David went to his suite. Jake and Sandy stood face to face.

"I don't know exactly what love is," Jake said taking hold of her hands. "I know I like you and care for you. I'd like to kiss you goodnight if…"

Before he could finish asking, Sandy leaned into him and they kissed, a gentle and loving kiss. Tingles went up and down his spine. He held her tight in his arms. Looking into her eyes he said, "Wow."

She smiled and said, "That was nice."

After another hug they parted and said goodnight. Walking to his room Jake knew he wanted Sandy to be a permanent part of his life. He also knew marriage would need to wait until after high school and USAFA.

"Lord, I've got a lot to talk with you about."

The next two days flew by. Three friends shared their thoughts and dreams around eating and shopping and site seeing. David busied himself with insurance claims and banking and boat shopping. The crescendo event came at nine o'clock Saturday evening when Sam dropped Jake and Sue at the airport hangar for their return flight to Oahu.

David gave Sue a hug and said, "Thank you and

your father for these past two days. Thank you for your friendship. I think you've become like a sister to Sandy."

Sue smiled. "I'm glad to have you both in my life."

She walked over to talk with Sandy and Jake. Mr. Yang came out of the hangar and greeted them all.

"I'm so happy for your rescue," Mr. Yang said shaking David's hand. "Sandy, you must be an amazing young woman to have captured the hearts of these two, as you have. I hope you will both accept the assistance of my company until you are able to get your affairs in order and resume your lives."

"You're very generous," David said. "Everything seems to be coming together. Another day or so and we'll be good."

"Excellent," Mr. Yang said. "Sue and Jake, we must proceed to customs. David and Sandy, God go with you."

Sue gave Sandy a hug, grabbed her bag and walked with her father.

David grabbed Jake in a fatherly hug. "You take care."

"I will."

Jake looked Sandy in the eyes. "I never want a good-bye to come between us." He pulled out a piece of paper with his cell phone number on it. "Here is my cell phone number. As soon as you get a phone, send me a text or email. Then I'll text or email you every day."

They hugged and kissed each other on the cheek. Jake grabbed his backpack and ran after the Yangs before his emotions got the better of him. A strong breeze came up behind him.

If I didn't know better, I'd say Cal provided a bit of

a breeze to move me along toward the hangar. Jake grabbed the hangar door but found it stuck. *Ace must be the cause of that.* He turned, glanced back and smiled at Sandy.

Right on cue she ran to Jake and kissed him. Jake dropped his bag and put his arms around her in a loving embrace.

"I love you, Sandy."

"My kiss will give you something more to remember me until I see you again. I've never felt this way about anyone. I love you, Jake."

He picked up his bag, grabbed the door handle and pulled the door open. "Text me," he said, walking through the doorway into the hanger.

"I will."

The door closed behind Jake, as he met up with Sue and Mr. Yang. Clearing customs the three boarded the jet and settled in for takeoff.

Jake closed his eyes. *Lord, I have high school to finish, the academy, pilot training, the Space Force and astronaut training. That's a lot of separation time for Sandy and me. Please help us navigate it all in a way that pleases You.*

Then he heard a whisper in his ear. "Remember." *Mic.*

"I say to you that likewise there will be more joy in heaven over one sinner who repents…" Luke 15:7

Acknowledgements

Thank you to my wife, **Judith Ann**, who is always with me as we navigate the ups and downs of life; to **Jennifer** my proofreader for grammar and content; and to **Cynthia** for encouraging me to improve my writing skill.

Richard Wolfram brings forty-two years of ministry experience as a Lutheran pastor and thirty years of military experience, from cadet to crew chief to chaplain, together to produce stories that connect theology, military experience, leadership and youth dynamic into realistic stories of Christian faith and life. His books aimed at fourteen to sixteen-year-old boys have strong female characters too. The books will appeal to parents and grandparents looking for Christian-oriented books for their children and grandchildren. He and his wife, Judy, reside in Michigan near their children and grandchildren.